The Litter of the Law

The Litter of the Law

A MRS. MURPHY MYSTERY

RITA MAE BROWN
& SNEAKY PIE BROWN

Illustrated by Michael Gellatly

BANTAM BOOKS

NEW YORK

Copyright © 2013 by American Artists, Inc.

Published in the United States by Bantam Books,
an imprint of The Random House Publishing Group,
a division of Random House LLC,
a Penguin Random House Company, New York.

BANTAM BOOKS and the HOUSE colophon are registered trademarks of
Random House LLC.

Illustrations copyright © 2013 by Michael Gellatly

LIBRARY OF CONGRESS CATALOGING-IN-PUBLICATION DATA
Brown, Rita Mae.
The litter of the law : a Mrs. Murphy mystery / Rita Mae Brown &
Sneaky Pie Brown ; Illustrated by Michael Gellatly.
pages cm
ISBN 978-0-345-53048-6 (alk. paper)
eBook ISBN 978-0-345-53857-4
1. Haristeen, Harry (Fictitious character)—Fiction.
2. Murphy, Mrs. (Fictitious character) —Fiction.
3. Women detectives—Virginia—Fiction. I. Title.
PS3552.R698L58 2013
813'.54—dc23
2013007940

Printed in the United States of America on acid-free paper

www.bantamdell.com

2 4 6 8 9 7 5 3 1

First Edition

Book design by Diane Hobbing

For
Kathleen King
Who knows the past is always with us.

Cast of Characters

Mary Minor Haristeen—"Harry," just forty-one, a Smith graduate who wound up being Crozet, Virginia's, postmistress for six-
teen years, is now trying to make some money by farming. She
survived breast cancer and prefers not to think about it. She more
or less lives on the surface of life until her curiosity pulls her
deeper.

Phararond Haristeen, D.V.M.—"Fair" specializes in equine re-
production. After graduating from Auburn he married his childhood sweetheart, Harry. He reads people's emotions much better
than his wife does. He is a year older than Harry.

Susan Tucker—Outgoing, adept at any and all social exchange,
she's Harry's best friend since cradle days. She loves Harry but
worries about how Harry just blunders into things.

The Very Reverend Herbert Jones—A Vietnam veteran, Army,
he is pastor at St. Luke's Lutheran Church, which is well over two
hundred years old. He is a man of deep conviction and feeling.
He's known Harry since her childhood.

Deputy Cynthia Cooper—Tall, lean, and Harry's next-door
neighbor as she rents the adjoining farm, she loves law enforcement. Harry meddles in Cooper's business from time to time but

the Smith graduate has an uncanny knack of finding important information.

Tazio Chappars—She's an architect in her early thirties often assisted by her yellow Lab rescue, Brinkley. Italian African heritage gives her dazzling good looks. She hails from St. Louis, Missouri.

Buddy Janss—A huge fellow and a successful farmer; he can be counted on to pitch in for fund-raisers. He and Harry like to discuss crops, weather, and new equipment.

Hester Martin—A middle-aged graduate of Mary Baldwin, she runs a roadside produce stand. Odd, opinionated, but blessed with a good heart, she drags people into her projects.

Aunt Tally Urquhart—This 101-year-old aunt of Marilyn Sanburne, Sr., does what she wants when she wants. She's not in too much evidence in this volume, which gives everyone a rest.

Marilyn Sanburne, Sr.—"Big Mim," known as The Queen of Crozet. She runs everything and everyone except her aunt. Big Mim is a political animal.

Marilyn Sanburne, Jr.—"Little Mim" has just had a baby, Roland. Her mother doesn't like the name. Often Little Mim doesn't like her mother.

Miranda Hogendobber—A second mother to Harry, a devout member of the evangelical Church of the Holy Light, she, too, isn't much in evidence in this volume. Like Big Mim, she's in her seventies and has no idea how she got there so fast.

Sheriff Rick Shaw—The sheriff of Albemarle County, he is over-burdened, underfunded, and overworked. Despite that, he likes law enforcement and has learned to trust Cooper. Originally, he wasn't thrilled having a woman in the department.

Neil Jordan—The treasurer for St. Luke's, Neil can be picky, picky, picky. He drives Harry crazy and vice versa but they have to work together as both are on the vestry board. He owns a fertilizer business that is lucrative.

Wesley Speer—He's also on the vestry board and brings a business perspective. He works sometimes with Neil since Wesley owns an upscale realty firm. He'll often refer clients to Neil. Wesley, like any high-end Realtor, is slick.

BoomBoom Craycroft—Another childhood friend of Harry's, she had an affair with Harry's husband years back. It was a mess, of course. Everyone has recovered and in many ways is the better for it. BoomBoom runs her late husband's concrete business. She is conventionally beautiful.

Alicia Palmer—Now here's a showstopper. Alicia was a movie star in the fifties, whipped through a few husbands, affairs, etc., made pots of money, inherited more from an old flame. She returned to Crozet, fell in love with BoomBoom, and is blissfully happy.

Sarah Price—Hester Martin's niece comes up to Crozet from Houston.

Paul Diaz—Tazio's boyfriend, who trains Big Mim's horses.

The Really Important Characters

Mrs. Murphy—She's a tiger cat who is usually cool, calm, and collected. She loves her humans, Tucker the dog, and even Pewter, the other cat, who can be a pill.

Pewter—She's self-centered, rotund, intelligent when she wants to be. Selfish as this cat is, she often comes through at the last minute to help and then wants all the credit.

Tee Tucker—This corgi could take your college boards. She is devoted to Harry, Fair, and Mrs. Murphy. She is less devoted to Pewter.

Simon—He's an opossum who lives in the hayloft of the Haristeens' barn.

Matilda—She's a large blacksnake with a large sense of humor. She also lives in the hayloft.

Flatface—This great horned owl lives in the barn cupola. She irritates Pewter, but the cat realizes the bird could easily pick her up and carry her off.

Shortro—A young Saddlebred in Harry's barn who is being trained as a foxhunter. He's very smart, young, good-natured.

Tomahawk—Harry's older Thoroughbred. They've been friends a long time.

The Lutheran Cats

Elocution—She's the oldest of the St. Luke's cats and cares a lot about the "Rev," as his friends sometimes call the Very Reverend Herbert Jones.

Cazenovia—This cat watches everybody and everything.

Lucy Fur—She's the youngest of the kitties. While ever playful, she obeys her elders.

The Litter of the Law

1

*F*air Haristeen, doctor of veterinary medicine, and his wife, Mary Minor "Harry" Haristeen, loved to steal a Saturday and cruise the back roads of central Virginia. It reminded them of their courting days, back in high school, when Fair, bruised from Friday night's football game, would pick up Harry, dirty from the stable, and they'd drive around in his 1958 Chevy pickup. Now, over two decades later, Fair was at the wheel of their station wagon, Harry beside him, the pets in the back seat, as they rode through the countryside.

Mrs. Murphy, the tiger cat, Pewter, her gray, overweight sidekick, and Tucker, the corgi, usually accompanied their people everywhere except in high heat. On a mild day like today, windows down a crack, the three could sleep or chat while the humans talked.

"Perfect weather," Fair declared.

October 12 was indeed a ravishing fall day—early fall, for the summer warmth lingered late this year. Forests looked spray-painted with yellow, orange, flaming red, deep red, old gold.

"Hey, Miranda got the respiratory flu." Harry mentioned a former co-worker and dear friend. "She's swearing that drinking electrolytes will cure her. She saw it on TV."

Fair shook his head. "Electrolytes will help, but our beloved Miranda seems susceptible to quacks."

Watching the passing scenery, Pewter noticed a lovely yellow clapboard farmhouse. "*Quack—duck. Why call a crook a quack?*"

"*I don't know,*" Tucker replied. The corgi was well used to Pewter's inquiring mind. "*They also use the term 'snake oil.' A quack sells snake oil. It's confusing.*"

"Ha!" Pewter whooped. "*If they'll buy snake oil, maybe we can get them hooked on catnip.*"

"*Humans don't sniff catnip,*" Tucker replied with dignity.

"*They can learn.*" The gray cat spoke with conviction.

"*Pewter, sometimes I think you're cracked as well as fat,*" the dog unwisely said.

"*Fat!*" Pewter raged.

"*You need a seat all your own. Every time we take a turn, the flab on your belly sways,*" Tucker teased.

Pewter lashed out, a quick right to the shoulder.

Tucker growled, showing her fangs.

"That is enough!" Harry turned around.

"*I haven't done a thing.*" Mrs. Murphy distanced herself from the combatants, who now rounded on her.

"*Brown-noser!*" Pewter whacked the tiger cat, who gave as good as she got.

The hissing and barking irritated Fair to the point where he pulled over to the side of the road, near where Hester Martin's vegetable and fruit stand was located.

Harry got out of the car, opened the back door. "I am going to give you such a smack."

All three animals jumped to the far back of the Volvo station wagon. Harry walked around to the rear of the car and opened the hatch door; the animals jumped back into their original seats.

Slamming both doors shut, Harry cursed as Fair couldn't help but laugh. She walked over to the driver's side; he had the window down.

"They know how to pluck your last nerve," said Fair, laughing.

"Yours, too. I'm not the one who pulled the car over." Harry looked down the road at the produce stand, a small white clapboard building with a large overhang, goods displayed in orderly, colorful rows. "Hey, let's get some pattypan squash. Bet Hester still has some." She walked around the car, getting in the passenger side before turning to face her animal tormentors. "If I hear one peep, one sniff, one hiss while I am shopping, no food tonight. Got it?"

"*Hateful.*" Pewter turned her back on Harry.

As Tucker hung her head, Mrs. Murphy, the tiger cat, loudly defended herself. "*I didn't do one thing.*"

"*Of course not, the perfect puss.*" Pewter curled her upper lip.

Fair coasted to the stand, where Hester—orange apron, black jeans, and an orange shirt—was talking to customers, most of whom lived in Crozet or nearby.

"I'll stay here." Fair knew how Hester could go on, plus Buddy Janss was there, all three hundred pounds of him, and he could outtalk Hester.

Orange and black bunting festooned the roof overhang. Scarecrows flanked the outdoor wooden cartons overflowing with squashes, pumpkins, every kind of apple imaginable. Inside, one could buy a good sandwich. Little ghosts floated from the rafters; big green eyes glowed in the room's upper corners. Brilliantly gold late corn and huge mums and zinnias added to the color.

Almost as big as Buddy, a sign sat catty-cornered to the entrance, announcing the community Halloween Hayride to raise money for the Crozet Library. No doubt Tazio Chappars, an architect, had designed the impressive sign. She worked hard for the library and the sign really grabbed you: From a large drawn skeleton, one bony arm actually reached out to get your attention.

Hester looked up. "Harry Haristeen, I haven't seen you in weeks."

Buddy turned. "How'd you do with your sunflowers?"

Buddy, a farmer who rented thousands of acres along with cultivating his own holdings, enjoyed Harry's foray into niche farming. Who knew better than Buddy the cost of equipment and implements for wheat, corn, soybeans? Harry had made a wise choice in focusing on her field of sunflowers, her quarter acre of Petit Manseng grapes, and the ginseng she grew down by the strong deep creek that divided her property from the old Jones farm.

"Pretty good," she said, not wanting to brag that this year's field of sunflowers was her biggest yet. "How's your year so far?"

He hooked his thumbs in his overalls. "Tell you what, girl, that mini-drought thinned out my corn crop. I did better than most because my lower acres received enough rain. Others didn't. Never saw anything like it. On one side of the road the corn would be twisted right up, and on the other just as plump as you'd please. The corn behind the old schoolhouses looks poorly."

Hester jumped in. "Government's fault. All that stuff they have circling around up there in space. Gotta affect us."

Both Harry and Buddy nodded politely, for Hester was a little in space herself. Sometimes a lot out there. Middle-aged, good-looking, with glossy light brown hair hanging to her shoulders, she applied just enough makeup to draw attention to her symmetry and health. Every small town as well as big city has its Hesters, it's just they can't hide in the small towns. Good-looking people, often bright, but they don't quite fit in and often they never marry. Hester had gone to Mary Baldwin, excelled in her studies, but came back over the Blue Ridge Mountains to run this roadside stand. Her brother, more ambitious, moved to Houston right out of the College of William and Mary. He had perfect timing, hitting Texas on the cusp of a building boom and making the most of it. Her parents had built the stand more as a hobby than a business, but it flourished. Her father had been a banker; her mother had run the stand. These days Hester seemed happy enough, engaged with a steady stream of regulars and tourists.

Buddy kindly semi-agreed. "What scares me is what we don't know. I mean, just in general, look at this drought and, hey, we came out a lot better off than they did in the Midwest, where everything burned up. Right now our water table is good. I planted more Silver Queen corn because I think the weather will stay warm longer. I'll get it harvested and if not, I'll make a lot of critters happy." He let out a booming laugh.

Hester asked, "You've got crop coverage, Buddy? After the drought of 1988, surely you started paying for an insurance policy, revenue protection."

"I do. I elected an eighty percent revenue protection policy. Yes, I did learn from 1988 but, girl, every time I turn around I'm writing another check and I see my return diminish. Farming gets harder and harder," said the well-organized man, a true steward of the land. "Just to keep up, I have to plant more acreage. Plant an early crop, then come back and throw soybeans down. I feel like I'm running to stay in place."

"Think we all do," Hester agreed.

"Only way I can buy or rent—and renting makes sense in the short term—is to sell some of my land closer in to Crozet or Charlottesville."

Hester's shoulders snapped back. "Don't do that, Buddy. Don't ever do that."

"Before I forget, Hester, do you have any pattypan squash?" Harry didn't want to keep Fair or the arguing animals in limbo.

"I do. Wait until you see it." Hester nodded to Buddy, who winked at Harry.

The two women walked inside, where there was crooknecked squash, acorn squash, and Harry's favorite, cream-white pattypan squash that looked like scalloped discuses.

"Beautiful! And the right size."

"Right about now the pattypan is usually over, but this year with the long, long summer, I'm still getting some," said Hester. "The melons are over, though. I do so love melons. Before I forget, now, you and Fair are buying tickets for the hayride. You must. The library is built but there's a lot to be done. We need $59,696 just for adult computers and, oh my, the adult area needs tables and we need furniture for a meditative reading room. The list is endless."

"Of course we'll buy tickets. I'll even buy tickets for Mrs. Murphy, Pewter, and Tucker."

"If that gray cat of yours gets any fatter, I'll have to find a special wagon and pony just for her." Hester laughed.

"You're looking pretty Halloweeny yourself, all orange and black."

"Oh, this is just my warm-up. Next week I'll be out here in my witch's costume."

"So long as you don't scare customers away."

"I could be a Halloween fairy except I've never seen a Halloween fairy."

They kept chatting as Harry picked out two succulent squashes, then paid at the cash register run by Lolly Currie, a young woman looking for a better job but making ends meet at Hester's stand until then.

Back on the road, Fair grinned. "That is the shortest time you have ever spent at Martin's Stand."

"Buddy Janss helped me out, because as soon as I paid for my squash, he came back to chat up Hester, about late produce deliveries. I swear, Buddy has put on more weight. His chins now have chins."

"Buddy may be fat but he's light on his feet. He was a hell of a football player in high school and college. It's a pity that retired linemen run to fat so often."

"Boxers, too." She watched rolling hills pass by.

"*Maybe you should go live with Buddy. The two of you could be Team Tubby.*" Tucker knew this would start a fight.

"*Don't,*" Mrs. Murphy counseled in vain.

"*Bubble Butt. Poop Breath!*" Pewter hissed loudly.

Harry twisted around in the front seat just in time to see Pewter hook the dog's shoulder with one claw.

"*Ouch,*" Tucker yelped.

"*Next, your eyes.*"

"Pull over, honey. There will be fur all over the car if I don't stop this right now."

He pulled over on the side of the road. The field on the north side of the two-lane road was jammed with corn. Morrowdale Farm usually put these fields in good hay, but this year row after row of healthy corn filled them. They had somehow escaped the small drought.

Opening the door to again castigate the backseat passengers, Harry remarked, "This has to be one of the best-run and prettiest farms in Albemarle County."

"Sure is."

They looked out to the scarecrow in the middle of the field, currently being mobbed by crows.

"I thought scarecrows were supposed to frighten crows," Fair said.

"Those crows are having a party. Look at that. Pulling on the wig under the hat." Harry laughed. "What are all those birds doing?"

Fair stepped out of the car to stare intently as a crow plucked out an eyeball.

"Honey, that's not a scarecrow."

2

"Tucker, come back!" Harry called to the corgi as the dog raced across the cornfield.

Fair, in his shock, hadn't closed the station wagon door, so all three animals had rushed out after deciding to see what was going on.

The corn rustled as the strong little dog bounded through.

The two cats also sped down a row, curiosity raging.

"Selective hearing." Harry shook her head as she followed, starting into a corn row.

"Honey, they'll be back. You should stay where you are, otherwise you might destroy footprints or some other kind of evidence."

She stopped, turned to face her husband. "You're right."

"I'm not sure you want to see the corpse anyway."

Harry leaned up against the Volvo. "Death really is ugly and this one is probably especially so. But, Fair, why truss someone up like a scarecrow?"

He folded his arms across his chest. "Clever, really. How many people passed by this field on Garth Road? Plenty, I bet, and still no one stopped or called the sheriff's department. The only reason we did was because of the ruckus raised by our passengers, and then the crows caught our eye, and . . . well."

As the married couple waited for the sheriff's department to arrive, the three investigating animals reached the base of the scarecrow.

A blue-black crow perched on the straw hat looked down. "*Beat it!*" he squawked.

Mrs. Murphy knew she could climb the dead man's leg if need be, so she stood on her hind legs reaching far up, feeling the cold flesh under the faux scarecrow's pants. "*I can climb up and shoo all of you away,*" she threatened the birds.

A second crow in this mob, on an outstretched arm, gibed, "*Go ahead. We'll fly away, circle, and come right on back.*"

The first crow opened his wings to their full span, the light picking up the blue highlights. "*What do you want with this feast? Cats don't eat carrion.*"

Pewter ignored the question and asked one of her own: "*Did you see the scarecrow being set up?*"

The second crow spoke. "*No, but he hasn't been here long. We caught a whiff as we flew over this cornfield on our way to Shelford Farm. When we tear off a juicy piece of meat, some blood still drips.*"

Few scarecrows are well dressed. Neither was this one. It wore a drab, wrinkled shirt over a red undershirt. Worn, old pants, rope for a belt, took care of his bottom half. Old work boots, the sole separated from the left one, covered his feet. The straw hat, edges frayed, hatband missing, gave the fellow the final country touch.

As blood pools in the extremities, the crows provided valuable information. The scarecrow wouldn't show the signs of rigor mortis because the body was tied, arms outstretched, legs tied down, too. No blood was moving, the body temperature had cooled down, but this was a fresh kill, relatively.

Mrs. Murphy noticed that the eyes had been plucked out and a lot of flesh had already been eaten off his face and hands. Eventually, the crows would have torn through the clothing.

"Did you smell another human?" the tiger cat asked.

"No. The sun had been up about an hour. What we smelled was him," the first crow reported, his olfactory powers acute, especially for blood and meat.

"Without his eyes, I can't tell if he was strangled," Pewter matter-of-factly announced. "They'd be bulging and bloodshot."

"Eyes are so tasty." A smaller crow opened his beak wide. "A real delicacy."

"Any idea how he was killed?" asked Mrs. Murphy.

"You didn't hear him scream, did you?" Pewter, normally not interested in much besides her own meals, was oddly thrilled at having discovered such an unusual murder.

"How could we have heard him scream?" a young crow replied. "He was dead and gone by the time we found him."

"Eat what you can, because the sheriff is on his way. He'll cut him down," Mrs. Murphy advised.

Tucker sniffed the bottom of the stake, sniffed the corpse's shoes, then picked up the diminishing odor of a set of rubber boots. Raising her nose, she sensed the smell moving away from the body, then, nose to ground, she began to track, the cats in her wake. As the three friends stuck to their trail of the pair of rubber boots, presumably those of the person who had carried the body, the crows burst out singing a song whose refrain was "Oh, those beautiful eyes, those great big beautiful eyes." Then they burst into raucous laughter.

"Gross," Tucker said.

"Yeah." Pewter looked back. "Twisted. They're really twisted."

"It's the killer who's twisted," Mrs. Murphy sensibly replied as she, too, kept her nose down.

The three followed the line until it came out to the side of the road, where there was a small stain that smelled like motor oil.

"*Every third person wears rubber boots around here when it's wet.*" Tucker sat down. "*But I think this is the spot where the scarecrow's companion parked, then carried out his body from here.*"

"*A strong person. They don't call it dead weight for nothing,*" Mrs. Murphy noted.

"*She's red in the face,*" Pewter said, referring to Harry, calling their names in the distance with increasing frustration. "*We'd better go back to the wagon.*"

When they got back to the Volvo, Harry scooped them up, put them in the back, and closed the door. "Curiosity killed the cat," she huffed, unaware of the irony of Harry Haristeen making such a statement.

"*Yeah, yeah.*" Pewter put her paws on the window just to make a smear.

"*She's upset.*" Tucker put her head on her paws.

"*Pop is, too. Humans can't face death.*" Pewter was right about that.

"*This is murder. Worse.*" Mrs. Murphy heard cars coming closer.

"*I found a head in a pumpkin, remember?*" Pewter reminisced.

"*We've heard that story a hundred times,*" Tucker grumbled, heading her off. "*This is just as weird. And we were first on the scene. I mean, after the crows and the killer.*"

The sheriff's car rolled up. Sheriff Rick Shaw stepped out from the driver's side and Deputy Cynthia Cooper emerged from the other. Cooper—Harry never called her Cynthia—rented the farm next to Harry's farm, the old Jones homeplace. The two women had become friends.

The two law enforcement officers carefully pushed through the late-maturing corn, the leaves rattling, ears full on the stalks. They looked downward as they walked but were rows away from the footprints that Tucker had found.

Harry and Fair stayed with their station wagon as instructed. They could see how carefully Rick and Cooper looked about, conferred, looked down. Then the two circled the scarecrow. The crows flew in loops around them.

One crow dive-bombed. *"Leave us alone!"*

Cooper ducked, then waved her hands at the noisy birds. "Damn."

Rick, tempted to take out his sidearm and fire, did not. No need to alert the residents of Morrowdale or anyone else at this moment.

After twenty minutes, they returned.

"Do you know who it is?" Harry asked.

Cooper shook her head. "The face is pretty well gone. But he's youngish, and had been in fairly good shape. Look, why don't you two go on home? I'll get a statement from you later. If there's anything of immediate importance, tell me now. Otherwise, you'll get caught up in the removal team, the forensic team, and, of course, the news team, as they know where we are every minute thanks to being able to listen in to all our calls."

Tucker barked from the car. *"There's a drip of oil just up the road. And footprints in a corn row."*

"Save your breath," Pewter, paws on the windowsill, counseled.

"They'll find the footprints," Mrs. Murphy said. *"The humans will crawl over that cornfield and the two of them will be down at Morrowdale questioning everyone and going through the barns and sheds."*

Harry and Fair drove west down Garth Road, then turned toward Crozet, heading south. The Blue Ridge Mountains were now on their right. They passed a large cattle farm, Dunrovin, with Herefords in the pastures; they passed by rolling acres of grapes, the land dotted here and there with old farmhouses and the occasional new structure, always sited for the view.

"You okay?" Fair asked.

"Yeah. You?"

"Yeah." They passed the apple shed now housing Chuck Pinell's leather shop. "Yeah, but . . ." His voice trailed off.

"Creepy." Harry shivered.

"People kill for lust, for love, in a fit of anger, or for money, and some because they are plain nuts," Fair said.

"You'd need to be pretty demented to take someone you've just killed and tie them up as a scarecrow, especially with Halloween just around the corner," Harry said. "Or it could be a side show designed to cover up another crime. Think about it."

Fair couldn't take his eyes off the road, because it was two-lane and treacherous. "I'd rather not." As he continued, his voice was firm, for his wife was more curious than the cats. "You don't need to think that much about it either. It was a shock. An unfortunate discovery. We can say a prayer for the victim and then go about our business."

"Prayers are wonderful. So are results. Who speaks for an innocent victim? Until I know more, I'm assuming he's innocent."

Knowing he was losing the battle against his wife's curiosity, he calmly replied, "Just leave this to Rick and Cooper."

"Of course."

"*Boy, was that a fib.*" Pewter giggled.

The others laughed with her.

Harry then said, "Whoever did it has quite the imagination."

"The last thing this county or state needs is an imaginative killer," said Fair, "especially if you're one of the victims."

"Fair, think about this: Don't most murderers try to dispose of their victim's bodies so no one finds them? Or if it's a crime of anger or passion, they run away and leave it, but they don't turn the corpse into a scarecrow or a public display. Whoever did this had time to plan it out."

"I guess."

"So I don't think it's a crime of passion."

"Unless the killer meant to make a mockery of the corpse." Fair braked at the stop sign at the Amoco station in Crozet. "Dammit. Now you've got me thinking about it. Let's just let it all go."

"Mmm." Harry was already off and running.

3

On the kitchen table, Pewter flopped on her side, her tail gently swaying. She thought this her best angle. Mrs. Murphy and Tucker thought otherwise.

As Harry opened the oven door to pop in a casserole, Pewter lifted her head.

"*I know you're making that for me.*" Her voice hit the dulcet-tone register.

Mrs. Murphy and Tucker, each curled up in their faux-sheepskin-lined animal beds by the door to the back porch, observed with amusement.

Mrs. Murphy imitated the gray cat's voice: "*I am the most loving kitty in the world.*"

Pointedly ignoring this, Pewter again sweetly meowed. "*I could use a little tuna until the casserole is ready.*"

Harry closed the door, set the timer, then turned to behold the cat, whose head was now raised, tail moving a bit faster. "Does smell good, doesn't it, Pewts?" Harry said. She caressed the cat's silken fur.

"*I have suffered a terrible shock,*" Pewter panted, pushing her head into Harry's hand. "*The sight of a shredded face. Crows devouring human flesh* before being impertinent to me. If one of those vile birds had dropped even two feet, I could have leapt up and torn it to bits."

"You're laying it on a little thick." The dog raised her head.

"Shut up, Bubble Butt. If she breaks out the cookies, you owe me big-time." Pewter rolled onto her back, cocking her head to one side.

"All right." Harry opened the treat cabinet, counted out two greenies, and gave them to Tucker. Next she opened a bag of cat treats in the shape of fishes. She gave half of these to Pewter, then walked over and gave the rest to Mrs. Murphy.

"You owe me!" Pewter cried in triumph as she gulped her tiny yellow fish.

Harry—unaware of the exchange, it sounded like meows and catcalling to her—walked back to her husband's small office in the old farmhouse.

"Forty-five minutes," she told him.

"Huh." He looked up from the screen. "Okay."

"Work?"

Fair was the best equine veterinarian in central Virginia.

He smiled sheepishly. "No. That's the trouble with the Internet. Easy to get sidetracked."

"And?" She came up behind him, placing her hands on his broad shoulders.

Not an inch of fat on the man.

"Uh, well, I've been kind of reading about bizarre murders. This website has examples going back to the eighteenth century. Really weird things, like duels fought in costumes or heads put on London Bridge with fake crowns. I guess that's political. But here's one from Wisconsin in the 1850s that caught my eye: A guy would kill men for no particular reason, or at least one no one could find, and he'd put them in a boat, push it out onto Lake Michigan, and set it afire. A Viking funeral. His victims were all men he had admired."

"Sometimes I wonder when I hear or read these things whether anyone is normal."

Fair leaned back in his chair. "I guess that's debatable." He rolled his chair around to face her, the rollers clicking on the hardwood floor. "I guess I can't fuss at you. Sometimes I'm a little too curious myself."

She kissed his cheek. "Makes me feel better," she said, then headed to the kitchen.

He followed the wonderful aroma of her chicken casserole, her mother's recipe.

"That scent brings back so many memories," Harry said. "And, hey, Halloween is what, two and a half weeks away? More memories."

"*Heads in pumpkins,*" Pewter blathered.

Tucker listened, then put her head back on her paws. "*I thought they were about to discuss food. They'd be much better off focusing on things that matter rather than random corpses.*"

The tiger cat silently agreed as she left her own bed to curl up with the corgi.

Both animals felt the chill of premonition.

4

*T*he day after the grisly discovery, the temperature dropped twenty degrees and rains came. Like all farmers, Harry had a rain plan. There were the chores that one did no matter the weather, and then there were those set aside for downpours.

The tack room in the old barn doubled as her office. If she had fixed up an office in the house, she knew she'd bother Fair or vice versa. The tack room made sense plus she could smell the leather, the horses, and their sweet feed. She liked sitting in the old knotty-pine room, the size of two good stalls, twenty by twenty-four feet. One wall held saddle racks and bridle holders. Under those items rested her personal tack trunk, as well as her husband's. Each horse stall also had a tack trunk in front of it, carrying items Harry felt should be separated from the main tack room. And each tack trunk hid treats: dried apples, special horse cookies. When a lid was lifted, the nickering started.

At fifty-two degrees Fahrenheit, the temperature hit the perfect mark for the horses. Most of them were turned out in the rain, which was now steady but soft. Once on the other side of the equinox, Harry switched her schedule, bringing the horses in at night and turning them out during the day. Horses needed to move about.

Pewter, splayed out on Harry's tack trunk, which was covered with a lush saddle pad, had no such inclination. Tiny snores emitted from her body. Mrs. Murphy, wide awake, sat on the desk surface just inches from her human, who was trolling the Internet and considering seed purchases for the spring. If Harry ordered now, she would benefit with a ten percent discount from Southern States, the large supplier. She would always double-check with Augusta Co-op to see if those prices were better.

Brow furrowed, chin resting on her hand, Harry scrolled through various seed types as the tiger cat peered at the screen, too.

Tucker, knocked out in her plaid bed under the desk, was as oblivious as Pewter.

An old massive teacher's desk, painted hunter green, a tall wooden file cabinet, and two director's chairs as well as the wooden teacher's chair in front of the desk took up the space opposite the saddle wall.

"I can't believe this," Harry said to Mrs. Murphy. "They say they've developed a winter-resistant Bermuda grass and it's only $123.50 per hundredweight. First, I don't believe it. Second, that is an outrageous price. Bermuda grass isn't as good as alfalfa or orchard grass."

"Then why use it?" The cat had a practical turn of mind.

Hearing the clear meow, Harry looked into the bright green eyes. "I love you, pussycat."

"I love you, too," the cat replied as the attractive forty-one-year-old woman returned to her task.

"It's the terrible summers we're having, Murphy. That's what makes Bermuda grass useful. We now need some kind of forage that can withstand the heat and drought conditions. Unfortunately, it dies in the winter. It looks as though fescue, orchard grass, and timothy die in summer's searing heat, but they do not.

They burn off, or wilt. The pastures are brown, but with a bit of moisture or a snowy winter, those grasses pop back up. Of course, clover really holds water in nodules." She nattered on, captivated with grass crops, as she had been since she was a tiny girl following her father around the farm.

While not enraptured by grasses, legumes, or corn, the tiger cat proved a good listener. Corn appealed to her because it brought in mice, foxes, and other animals seeking the high calories. Then she remembered the scarecrow and the crows.

Both Harry and Mrs. Murphy looked up when they heard a motor, then a door slam. Harry hurried outside to catch whomever it was before they ran through the rain to the back door.

"Coop, I'm in the barn," Harry hollered.

The tall blonde deputy smiled and hurried into the barn. "Can you believe how much cooler it is all of a sudden?"

As she walked down the center aisle to the tack room, Harry replied, "October."

Once inside, Cooper sank into a director's chair. She leaned over to peer under the desk.

"So much for Tucker being a guard dog."

Harry laughed. "She really is dead to the world, isn't she?" Then she indicated the fat gray cat on the tack trunk. "Another one."

"You need to tie a roller skate under Pewter's stomach."

"Coop, that's a great idea."

Mrs. Murphy giggled.

"How was church this morning?" Cooper inquired. "I overslept."

"Herb gave a really good sermon, as always. He talked about harvesttime and read some passages from the New Testament about gathering. He always holds my interest."

"He makes it real. Not a bunch of rules." Cooper rented the

Reverend Herb Jones's homeplace, as the pastor of St. Luke's Lutheran Church had moved in to the beautiful vicarage on the church grounds.

"Can you imagine building St. Luke's? This used to be the Wild West. The Monacans"—Harry mentioned an Indian tribe—"weren't happy to see us."

"Still aren't, I bet," Coop said.

"Small wonder." Harry inhaled. "Anyway, Albemarle County didn't really start rolling until after the Revolutionary War. That's when the first stone was laid for St. Luke's. Don't you love the church building that evolved?"

"I do. I love people that evolve, too." Coop sighed.

"Okay, what's on your mind?" Harry knew her friend and neighbor well enough to tell from the tilt of the conversation that Coop was turning something over in her mind.

"University of Virginia football, for one. Every time there's a home game, it's one scrape after another, plus we have to really keep our eyes out for the kids who are flat-out loaded. Hey, I was in college once, too. I don't mind if you get drunk. Everyone has to learn that one, how to handle the bottle, but I don't want them behind the wheel of a car."

"That's not going to change. Do you know who the scarecrow is yet?"

"No. We found a class ring." Cooper leaned closer. "The crows had eaten the flesh from his fingers and hands. It slipped off. Actually, crows like shiny things. If we hadn't gotten there when we did, that Virginia Tech ring would be in a nest somewhere."

"Did it have initials and a year inscribed?"

"J.H., 1998."

"Did you find anything else?"

"Nothing. Pockets empty. But we'll get an ID soon enough.

Well, I speak too soon. But the faster you have an ID, the easier some links of inquiry are. For all we know, the killer is in Paraguay by now."

"I don't think so." Harry leaned forward.

"Actually, Harry, I don't either."

"I'll see that scarecrow forever. The sight itself was unpleasant enough, but the whole idea of it is really disturbing, you know?"

"I do." Cooper sat quietly for a moment. "Pewter snores."

"Yes, she does." Harry laughed.

"No one wants to sleep next to her," Mrs. Murphy informed them to no avail.

"Where's Fair?"

"He got an emergency call. Sometimes that man works around the clock. It's a good thing he loves what he does."

"Me, too," Cooper chimed in.

"The horrible part of police work, like finding a corpse scarecrow, doesn't get to you?" Harry wondered.

"I can't say that finding murder victims thrills me, but finding their killer does."

"You know I read the paper, magazines. There are articles claiming that there are identifiable traits in children who grow up to become violent. Some writers even suggest putting them away before a crime has been committed."

"Even if we could violate individual rights that way, there would still be murders," Cooper stated.

"The human condition?"

"Unfortunately, yes."

5

Pulling his veterinary truck up to the house that Sunday evening, Fair opened the truck's door, then got out and wearily leaned against it.

Tucker, hearing the motor, dashed out the house's animal door to greet him. "Hi, Pop. I missed you. I'm glad you're home."

The tall man bent down to pet the dog. "Hey, buddy."

"You're covered in blood and you're sad and tired. Can I help?" Tucker implored him with her soft brown eyes.

Fair stroked the smooth head once more before standing. Taking a deep breath, he walked to the house.

In the kitchen, Harry heard his footfall but didn't look up as she stuffed a Cornish hen. "First frost tonight, I think."

"Feels like it."

She turned and took in his bloodied, bedraggled appearance. "Oh, no! Honey, is the horse all right?"

He sank into a kitchen chair. "Couldn't save her. She'd nicked her aorta. By the time Paul Diaz found her out in the pasture, she'd already lost so much blood. What a beautiful filly." He rested his head in his hands. "The Medaglia d'Oro filly."

"Oh, no." Harry washed her hands. "Big Mim had such hopes for her."

Medaglia d'Oro was a Thoroughbred stallion with a big career. Even in these hard economic times, his stud fees had been creeping up, and Big Mim had selected a mare to breed to him. He'd been siring winners on the track. The Queen of Crozet, as she was called behind her back and even to her face, had a knack for breeding, whether for steeplechasing or flat racing. It ran in her family. Her mother had it, too, and Big Mim passed it on to her daughter, Little Mim, who had recently given birth to a boy. Perhaps the magic would pass to him.

"That filly was one of the most correct horses I've ever seen. We all thought she was bound for greatness."

Coming from Fair, that meant something.

"Is Big Mim okay?"

He thought a moment. "She's a horsewoman. She accepts fate. But she's upset. Seeing any animal you love die . . ." He shrugged.

Harry put her arms around him. "I know you did your best. I'm so sorry, honey."

"The poor girl was down in the pasture. She'd lost so much blood, she couldn't stand up, so I ran out, cleaned the wound, and she died while I was stitching her up. If she'd lived, I think we could have rolled her onto a canvas and dragged her into the barn, gotten her in a stall. I was prepared to give her massive transfusions and drip antibiotics into her. Whatever it took."

"Big Mim would have sat up with you." Harry warmed at the thought of the svelte septuagenarian sitting in the aisle, wrapped in a blanket.

"She would; Paul would, too. I think even Jim"—he named Big Mim's husband, who was not a horse person—"would have taken a turn."

"Me, too." She kissed him. "You are such a good veterinarian. Such a good man. I love that you care."

He kissed her hand. "Most of us do. A person should only go into medicine, veterinary or human, if they really care."

"Well, that's a subject for a long discussion, and my money is on the vets." She kissed his cheek again.

"Let me get out of these clothes, shower. I'll throw them in the washer."

"Fair, how did it happen?"

"No idea. Honestly, honey, if I knew how half my patients did the stuff they did to themselves, I would be a genius. Horses are pretty careful animals but they can do the dumbest things sometimes, and she was young." He smiled. "That doesn't help."

"Doesn't for us either." Harry stopped. "Except now that I am officially middle-aged, I pray the young will be a little wild, take some crazy chances, think the unthinkable."

He stood up. "You still do. Every now and then, I really have no idea what's going on upstairs." He tapped his head with his forefinger.

"*He's right*," Pewter, in her kitchen bed, remarked to Mrs. Murphy, who sprawled in Tucker's bed as the dog followed Fair out of the room.

"*Poor Fair*." Mrs. Murphy ignored Pewt's comment about Harry—not because it would start an argument, but because she knew it was true.

"*Tucker will cheer him up*," said Pewter.

"*We could, too*," said the tiger cat. "*We could take our catnip mouse in the bedroom and throw it around. Fair always laughs when we do that*."

Pewter was firm. "*I'm not getting out of this bed unless food is involved*."

"*Right*." Mrs. Murphy smiled at her friend.

Harry slid the two small Cornish hens into the oven. She'd made a salad earlier. Neither she nor Fair ate heavy rich foods and this would be a good supper for them. Also, Harry lacked the time to prepare complicated meals.

The wall phone rang.

She wiped her hands on a dish towel and picked it up. "Haristeen."

"Cooper."

"Hey, if you haven't eaten supper, come on back. I'll have plenty."

"Date tonight."

"You stopped by here and you didn't tell me that? I am wounded, deeply wounded," Harry teased.

"Forgot. It's a first date. We'll see. I'm just glad I have a night off. I've worked the last three weekends."

"The county really needs to hire more people, don't they?"

"No money. I called to tell you, since you and Fair found him: We have an ID on the scarecrow."

"That was fast."

"The ring really helped, and we have super people sitting behind those computers and making calls. I don't think people in the county have any idea how good their sheriff's department really is."

"It's kind of like making a will. No one thinks about it until they have to, I guess. So?"

"Joshua Hill, graduated from Tech in 1998. Accounting major. Worked for a large firm in Richmond for four years, then hung out his own shingle in Farmville, where he quickly built up a large clientele. Unmarried. Hobbies: fly-fishing, country music concerts."

"How did you get so much information so quickly?"

"Caitlin did," said Coop, referring to one of the criminologists on the staff, a fantastic researcher. "She went online, got the 1998 yearbook, and started looking. Even though our victim was torn up, we had a decent description of height, weight, approximate age, and hair color, and she narrowed it down to a few possibilities. Then she started calling places where the potential matchups worked. Josh didn't come into his office on Friday, nor did he call, which his assistant found odd but she wasn't overly concerned. I'm going down there Tuesday. Haven't seen Farmville in a long time, and I hear Longwood University has grown. It's a pretty school."

"Yes, it is." Harry paused. "Accountants don't get themselves murdered too often, do they?"

"No. This is a curious case."

"Who's the date?" Harry just had to know.

"Barry Betz, new batting coach for UVA. First year here. This guy has the sweetest smile. He lights up a room."

"Hope it's fun. I'd go out with him just because of his name." Harry smiled. "Thanks for calling me."

Fair walked in, clean, wearing a T-shirt and sweatpants. When he sat down, she told him about Josh, the dead accountant.

"Maybe he was cooking the books," said Fair, after devouring half of the Cornish hen Harry had cooked for dinner.

"If that's a motive, wouldn't there be so many more dead people in America, especially in certain professions and industries?" she remarked, gazing at him across the table.

"You've got a point there." Fair was feeling better and so was Tucker, wedged between his slippered feet.

"Sometimes I think about why people commit crimes, not the impulsive ones but the premeditated kind," Harry said. "I bet once you're free from society's rules or an ideology, anything is possible. The world is your oyster."

"Never thought of it that way." He stopped for a second. "This hen is wonderful."

"Oh, thanks. Miranda's recipe." Harry knew any recipe from

Miranda would be delicious. "It's kind of like offense and defense. The criminal is the offense, so that split-second advantage is his. He knows what he will do. The law has to react."

She neglected to add that the law could only react if they knew what was going on.

"I ought to arrest you, throw the book at you!" Cooper shouted at Harry two days later, on the street outside Joshua Hill's office in Farmville.

"For what?"

"Stalking?"

"I came to shop. You have no grounds for suspicion."

The attractive police officer shook her head. "Harry, how can you look in the mirror after a lie like that?"

"Farmville is famous for its furniture warehouses. I especially like Number 9, so named since all the warehouses had numbers on the outside, easy to see. And come on, Coop, you know I've been wanting to get down here for months. It's been one thing after another."

Calmed down a bit, Cooper replied, "You didn't have to come today. You want to know what I found out at Hill's office, and it was a big zero."

"His assistant wouldn't talk?"

"No." The lean woman put her elbows on the hood of her unmarked car, called a slicktop. "She kind of just answers the phone. She has a million pictures of her grandchildren on her desk. It's fair to say she isn't overly involved in her work."

"But she did note that her boss hadn't called in?"

"Yes, but she also said a lot of times he worked at home, or he called on clients at their offices."

"Did she give you a client list?"

"Harry!"

"Hey, you wouldn't be on this case if I hadn't found the body." Though she knew this wasn't one hundred percent true, Harry still pressed her point. "And murder is a lot more exciting than picking up drunk frat boys who then puke all over the back of your squad car."

"No drunk has ever puked in my car."

"Now who's the liar?"

Cooper took out her service revolver. "I put this to their temple, and tell them if they throw up in my car, I will blow their brains out."

"I can see how that might work."

"One time," the cop mused, "I had to pull over 'cause a guy pretended he was going to be sick, and then he ran into the woods."

"What did you do?"

"Followed until he tripped and fell. It was pitch-black. Then he threw up. Drunks are truly disgusting."

"Mmm. Anything of interest in Hill's office?"

"You enter into a small waiting room. There are a few nature prints, both there and in his office. His desk didn't have a single paper on it. I'll get the Prince Edward County Sheriff's Office to go over it all." Cooper gave out just enough information to tease Harry.

"You'd think an accountant would have piles of papers on his desk," said Harry.

"Or some, anyway," Coop agreed. "Though clients send so much stuff through email."

"Was his computer in the office?"

"Yes. Obviously, I can't take it without jumping through all the proper legal hoops, but I've already set that in motion. A forensic accountant could find out if Hill was doing anything suspicious. Anything you put into a computer can be dug out. Best to not put it there in the first place. Of course, I don't know that this murder has anything to do with numbers. Truth is, I don't know what this murder is about at all. Usually, I get a hunch."

"Don't you want to know what I found in Number 9 warehouse?"

Cooper gave her a sharp look. "If you did find something, you'll complain about the price."

"Follow me."

Harry climbed back in her Volvo station wagon. She'd parked outside Hill's office once she'd cruised through her favorite warehouse so her excuse for being in Farmville wouldn't be a total fib.

"Why should I follow you to see furniture?"

"Cooper, please follow me."

Something in Harry's voice made Cooper close the door to the slicktop, turn the key, and tag behind her neighbor.

Once at the warehouse, Harry opened the showroom door for Cooper. "Ready?"

Cooper stepped inside and stood a moment. "This place is huge."

"Four big floors, I think. But what I want you to see is right here on the first floor, the flashy showroom floor."

Briskly walking, Harry reached the middle of the cavernous building. Pumpkins, mums, and Halloween witches overhead all drew attention to a stunning country kitchen with a solid oak table, easily seating twelve.

"Look."

Cooper followed Harry's forefinger to a figure in the corner of the display room, among ghosts, more pumpkins, and little goblins popping out of the pumpkins.

"Jesus." The officer whistled.

In the middle of this lively display was a scarecrow with a drab undershirt, old pants with a rope belt, worn-out work boots, the sole separating from the left one. A straw hat topped it off. An exact replica of Joshua Hill.

7

*S*quares of fabric and seed catalogues littered Cooper's desk at police headquarters. Peering at her computer screen, she scanned a list of clothing manufacturers.

Eyes watering, she clicked off her computer, got up, stretched, and went outside. She tapped out a long coffin nail, lit it, watched the sky shift colors.

Sometimes taking a smoke break cleared her mind. Along with an increased chance of lung cancer, she'd get better ideas. After a few thoughtful minutes, she ground out the stub, walked back in, tidied up her desk, and left for the day. She'd worked overtime this Tuesday but didn't mind.

Driving home, she noticed the last of the day birds returning to their nests. A few bats were already out and about. She liked bats; they kept the bug population down.

Thinking about bugs and pests snapped Coop back to this strange scarecrow case. After Harry had pointed out the unsettling look-alike dummy, Coop had sent her on her way, then had gone to the store's office and asked to see their display person. In Coop's mother's day, that individual would have been called a window dresser regardless of what part of the store they decorated.

The display person was named Melinda and the young lady worked in the store full-time. Well groomed, well spoken, she was well dressed, good-looking.

Cooper was good at relaxing people. She sat the light-blonde-haired woman down in the middle of one of her own displays. After a bit of chitchat, she asked Melinda about the scarecrow.

"Don't you love the boots?" she gushed. "They aren't as easy to find as you might think and . . ." She trailed off. "Sorry. I get enthusiastic about these things."

"No, no, that's fine. But did you work with anyone else on that particular display?"

"No. I do all the work here in Number 9. The guys help me move the furniture but that's it. Actually, I like that I can let my imagination go."

"Would you have any way of knowing if someone asked specifically about that scarecrow?"

"No. No one asked me, but, Officer Cooper, there's a great volume of foot traffic through these warehouses, especially on the weekends. People come from all over Virginia, even from out of state. Lots of volume."

"Did you have any particular inspiration for the clothing?"

The young lady thought for a moment. "No. I mean, just the scarecrows I saw as a child." She grinned. "Can't be a scarecrow without a big straw hat."

"Would you mind giving me a list of where you bought the pants, the shirt, the boots, and the hat?"

"Not at all. If you wait a minute, I can print it out for you." Melinda hurried to her office, returning to Cooper in ten minutes, just enough time for the deputy to see an end table she wanted.

"Thank you," Cooper said as she quickly perused the list Melinda had given her. "I guess anyone could buy this clothing."

"That's the idea." Melinda smiled.

Cooper smiled back. "I won't take up much more of your time. Did you know Joshua Hill?"

"No."

"Do you live in Farmville?"

"No. I live on the eastern edge of Buckingham County and drive in. I'd like to move down here when I can afford it. May I ask you a question? What's this about?"

"Friday, October 11, Josh Hill, who had an accounting business near here, was murdered in Albemarle County. His dead body was found on Saturday. It was a big football weekend. Didn't make the front page of the papers until Monday."

"That's horrible."

"He was dressed just like your scarecrow here."

Melinda's eyes popped. "How awful."

"Well, yes, but it must have been a lot of work to dress him up, I would think."

Melinda paused. "The straw man took me about an hour to get all the clothes on, then make a head, paint on features. He's not exactly scary or gruesome. I mean, a scarecrow isn't, but I think a human one would be awful. I wish I could help you, but anyone could have come in and seen my scarecrow, and the clothing isn't unique or anything."

"Well, I've taken up enough of your time." Cooper handed her her card. "If you should think of something or if someone as to come in here and seem really focused on your display, let me know."

"I will."

Later, Cooper replayed that conversation. She felt the young woman was telling the truth. It had been a shot in the dark, but that's what she did. Lots of shots in the dark, lots of scraps of paper, old receipts, chewing gum wrappers, computer records, if she could get them. The endless gathering of data, most of it useless. But it only takes one perfect clue to point you in the right direction.

After being sent home, Harry drove leisurely through Dillwyn, then west through Scottsville on Route 6. At Route 151 she turned right, right again on Route 250 to head home to Crozet. The late afternoon sun's magical light enhanced every field and stone wall, even those raggedy few gas stations on the way.

Tuesday, October 15, was just a gorgeous day, the kind that makes one forget the suffocating heat of summer or the soon-to-come frigid winter days.

Hester Martin's stand stood up ahead, decorated even more lavishly than usual. Two farm trucks were unloading produce and there stood Hester, in witch's costume, directing the men. Next to Hester a well-groomed black mini schnauzer kept an eye on the men.

Laughing, Harry parked in the lot.

"Woo woo," Harry called out as she got out of the car.

Hester turned and picked up her broom, to shake at her.

The deliveryman closest to Hester ducked.

"Olin, don't you dare drop one apple," she admonished the man.

Jake, in the bed of his truck, leaned over with another wooden crate of plump green apples. "You fly with that broom, Hester?"

"I've got my pilot's license," she sassed. Then, to Harry, she said, "Girl, you just go on and pick out whatever you want. I can't leave these boys for one minute. They need constant supervision. Heidi is helping." Hester indicated the schnauzer. "She belongs to my old friend Cindy Walters, who's around here somewhere."

Jake rolled his eyes, saying nothing.

The other fellow on the ground, Greg Perez, carefully carried pumpkins to a pile he was building. No point in having Hester cuss him out, plus she might give him a big tip.

Inside the other truck, his partner, Stafford Schikel, groaned as he lifted another major pumpkin. "Hester, these are the best pumpkins you've ever seen."

"Big," she replied simply. "Did you cheat and put grow dust on them?"

"No. You know we do everything organic. We lose a lot to worms, birds, and rats because of it and you." He grinned. "You only buy organic."

"You charge me enough." She hadn't put her broom back.

"You want organic pumpkins, you pay."

"Yeah. Yeah." She pushed her pointed hat a bit to the side. "You know I go by your fields, I get out and smell everything. I run my fingers over the skins."

"We know."

She'd told them this ad infinitum.

Olin picked up another apple crate and asked, "Ever find anything?"

"Not at either of your farms, but let us never forget the owner of the organic store in Charlottesville who got busted for lying. His stuff was no different than Food Lion's."

Greg couldn't help but tweak her. "Food Lion is a good company, and, Hester, not everybody can afford organic produce. It is more expensive."

"You are what you eat," she forcefully replied. "If you care about your body, you eat right. No processed foods. No foods that have suffered chemical sprays. That's that."

Harry joined the conversation. "Well, I am eating this fresh lettuce and I will buy one of your super pumpkins. Think I'll make a big jack-o'-lantern." She smiled.

"Fellas, excuse me." Hester walked back inside to the cash register.

Lolly Currie quickly put down her e-book reader.

"Now, girl," said Hester to Harry, "it's time to buy those hayride tickets." Hester reached next to the old cash register as Lolly slipped out two large glossy tickets decorated with an illustration of goblins riding on a hay wagon drawn by spectral horses. "Two?" Hester asked.

Lolly piped up: "We have lots."

"I bought my tickets," Harry reminded Hester, "but I'll see if I can sell some."

"Hmm. So you did."

"Shameless." Cindy Walters laughed as she pointed her forefinger at Hester. "You'll chain people to the pumpkin stand before you'll let them go without a ticket."

"Well." Hester blushed, then introduced Cindy. "Harry, this is Cindy Walters from Florida and this little tyke is Heidi."

"*Hello.*" The schnauzer barked.

"We met at an environmental conference years ago. Been friends ever since." Cindy checked the clock on the wall. "I'd better push off."

"Oh, stay the night," Hester offered.

"If I get into North Carolina I can make Florida the next day."

"Wait! You can't go without buying a Halloween Hayride ticket."

"And I want to buy your best pumpkin," Harry quickly interjected.

"I'll have Greg pick out the biggest and put it in your station wagon. How's the mileage on that?"

"Good," said Harry. "Of course, newer cars get even better."

"Save where you can so you can help the library." She grinned. "Our two-year book fund is $175,000."

Harry laughed. "Hester, you're relentless."

She nodded. "I know, but this is critical to not just Crozet but the western part of the county. For years Crozet was always the weak sister, but we're coming up. This library means a lot. Mike Marshall, the Crozet reporter, is coming on the hayride. You know he'll write about Mrs. Murphy, Pewter, and Tucker. Cindy, don't you dare walk out of here without a ticket."

Mike Marshall was the editor and publisher of the Crozet Gazette, so if he covered it, it was news.

"Hester, I'm touched that you remember my cats' and dog's names."

"Family." She exited with Harry. "Greg, pick the biggest and prettiest pumpkin for Harry."

"You bet."

Cindy walked with them, ticket in her hand.

Just then Buddy Janss pulled up front, crates of late sweet corn in the back of his well-used pickup. A minute later, he walked toward them.

Hester turned to Buddy and fired away: "How many acres of late-maturing sweet corn did you plant?"

"Just like I told you last week and the week before, I planted two hundred acres. And those cool September nights just make the late sweet corn taste like candy. I harvest it twenty days after the first silks appear, I put it in huge tanks of ice water, and I bring it to you."

"Mmm?" She raised her carefully plucked eyebrows. "Long, long summer. You were smart to plant so late."

"Well, I planted corn every two weeks throughout the summer, but I waited extra long for the Silver Queen. Read my Farmers' Almanac. Better than the National Weather Service." He grinned, revealing a slight gap between his front teeth, as he winked at Harry.

"Odd, isn't it?" Harry agreed. "I find the same thing and I read it every morning."

A few cars rolled by. One turned in, lured by the display.

"A new customer." Hester beamed as she walked over to welcome the young man.

Buddy shook his head, smiling. "She asks me the same thing again and again."

"Yep." Harry crossed her arms over her chest. "If there's one tiny deviation in your story or one of mine from one week to the other, she's like a chicken after a grub."

"Just her way." He shrugged his massive shoulders.

"Some people can't fully trust," said Harry. "They can like you but they can't accept what you tell them. They have to see it for themselves or check and double-check, just like Hester. Buddy, can you imagine how exhausting that is?"

"Never thought about it."

"Means you can't learn from other people, your world becomes very narrow. I guess I thought about it as a kid because I had a great-uncle like that. After all these years, I now believe that trust is the bedrock of a community and it's the only way we can progress. Each of us doesn't have to invent the wheel."

"Harry, how do you think of this stuff?" He took off his ball cap, revealing tightly curled jet-black hair.

"On my tractor. Bouncing along jogs my brain."

He chuckled. "I'm on my tractor more than you, and I think about how dry the soil is, what is the soil temperature, should I check it, and what's the chance of rain."

"Yeah, but your tractor is like a Rolls-Royce. Doesn't bounce." She grabbed his hand and squeezed it while they both had a laugh.

Hester returned just as Tazio Chappars drove onto the crushed-stone parking lot. Brinkley, her yellow Lab, sat in the car, with the windows rolled down.

Tazio, now in her early thirties, became more lovely with each year. Harry liked her very much but had to wonder what her secret was: great bone structure or an unerring fashion sense? Whatever it was, Harry felt she didn't have it, but she muddled along and in extremis would smack a full coat of makeup on her face. Fortunately, she, too, had good bone structure.

"Taz!" Harry waved as the gorgeous architect walked in. "It is true! Hester attracts the best people."

Under his breath, Buddy muttered, "And the most beautiful."

"Why, thank you, Buddy." Harry punched him lightly in the stomach.

"Violence! No violence at my stand." Hester joined in the fun.

"You look happy," Harry remarked to Taz.

"I just got the green light to redesign the Western Albemarle High School library." As she looked Hester's way, Tazio's gorgeous features displayed the beauty of her African Italian heritage. "And I thank you for that," she said.

The older lady smiled. "I didn't do a thing."

"Yes, you did. You fought for me to work on the new Crozet Library, and what a difference that has made in my career. I thought I'd be knocking out development houses forever and then I prayed I would be once the crash came. I can never repay you, Hester."

"Sure you can. Buy a pumpkin."

The neighbors and friends laughed, and Brinkley barked from the car, which set off Tucker in the Volvo.

More cars pulled in.

"Wow. Big day," Harry noted.

"I'd better go inside and help out Lolly at the cash register," Hester said. "She's easily overwhelmed."

With a pumpkin in the back of the Volvo, Harry smiled all the way home. She glanced in her rearview mirror to see Hester still talking to Cindy and Heidi. Obviously, the good woman hadn't made it back into her store nor could Cindy get in her car.

Later that evening, Cooper turned in to the driveway to Harry's farm. The lights were still on. She stopped her SUV at the barn just as Tucker rushed out to greet her. Both Harry's station wagon and Fair's truck were parked by the barn.

As Tucker accompanied her, she opened the screened porch door, then knocked on the kitchen door.

Within a minute, Fair, smiling, opened the door. "Hello, neighbor."

"Hi, Fair. Forgive me for not calling first."

"Are you just coming home from work?"

"Long day, but you know all about long days."

He nodded. "Madam is in the living room and I'm on my way to the barn, if you need me."

Cooper entered the simple well-proportioned room with high ceilings. The fireplace gave off an inviting scent: burning pearwood. The cats lounged on the back of the sofa.

Harry, board on her lap, was drawing.

Setting that aside on the coffee table, she asked, "Are you still mad at me?"

"No. I got over being mad at you when you showed me the scarecrow at Number 9."

"Any luck?"

The taller woman shrugged. "No, but I didn't expect the decorator to come at me with a meat-ax. She was quite nice, actually."

"Isn't that weird? I mean, the exact outfit."

"Yes, it is."

"So what's next?"

"Tracking down clients. Rick questioned everyone at Morrow-dale the day you and Fair found the body on their property. They were horrified, but no one had driven out that way, so they hadn't seen it. Everyone on the farm was questioned." She sat down across from her friend.

"You have a lot of patience," Harry complimented her. "You're dogged and determined."

"I have to be. I live next to you."

Harry laughed. "Hey, look at my little garden drawing. Maybe I'll get it right this time."

"You taught me to plan my garden in the fall or winter, and so I have. Along with trying to focus on this case, I'm going through the possibilities."

"Is there anything I can do to help?"

"With my garden, I can always use your help. With the case, I live in fear."

"I'm not that bad."

"*Yes, you are*," Mrs. Murphy said.

"Let's say you have a way of stumbling onto things like the Number 9 scarecrow today," said Coop. "What if the killer had been the decorator? Or someone in there observed you studying the scarecrow? Someone involved in this murder. You can't take chances like that."

Harry didn't reply.

"Harry?"

"I know you're right."

"*Knowing Cooper is right doesn't mean she'll stop*," said Pewter.

"We know so little," said Coop. "This could be a revenge kill-ing. If you dig enough into people's lives, you eventually find someone who can't stand them or someone who is unbalanced."

"Kind of scary," Harry mumbled.

"*Well, it's almost Halloween.*" Pewter giggled.

"I dug down a little deeper." Cooper crossed one leg over the other, pulled at her anklet to stretch her leg. "Hill loved fly-fishing. Had a two-thousand-dollar fly rod. How can a fishing rod cost that much?"

"Beats me." Harry held up her hands.

"*Me, too. I don't need one,*" Pewter bragged, lifting her head off her arm.

Tucker was astonished at such a bold-faced lie. "*What? You can't fish.*"

"*I didn't say I fished. I wait for Mom to open a can of tuna. Now, that's real fishing.*"

Mrs. Murphy laughed at her gray friend.

"Two thousand dollars." Cooper dropped her crossed leg. "Boxes of flies. He was very organized and had quite a few books on fishing, according to the team that searched his house today. Fishing was his passion in life, so it seems. On his computer we found what you would expect—a list of clients, a list of other accounting firms and legal firms as well as IRS agents for his area. Pretty cut and dried. Oh, one strange thing: Hester Martin's name. No tagline, nothing, just 'Hester Martin' and the farm stand address, phone number, and her email."

"Did you talk to Hester about him?"

"Drove over earlier today. She said she knew him some. He was a member of the Upper Mattaponi tribe. She seemed a little bit resentful at being questioned. I don't know. Maybe she was in a bad mood. That was the extent of it."

"Hester does attend those annual powwows. Every year she says she's going. Never says why or what happens." Harry thought a moment. "She's not a tribe member, but she's so interested in proper use of the land, I think that's the real draw."

Cooper furrowed her brow. "She told me she's always had an

interest in the Virginia tribes. Her mother was a Sessoms, which is a Cherokee name."

Harry drew a long breath. "That's right. I think my mother once mentioned it back when I was in fifth grade."

"How can you remember fifth grade?"

"Because that's when we learn about the peoples who were here before we came. I loved it."

"Anyway, that was that. Hester was shocked that such a nice fellow, as she put it, was killed. As far as she knew, he wasn't a crook. Said Josh Hill always treated her kindly."

"Coop, did you know there are eleven Virginia tribes?"

"I do now. I started looking this stuff up to see if there might be any connection at all to Hill's bizarre death. It's terrible."

"His murder, sure," Harry responded.

"No. The way the Virginia tribes are pushed around. The Commonwealth only recognizes eight tribes and the federal government doesn't recognize Virginia tribes at all. It really stinks."

"That and much else." Harry sighed. "I guess the feds didn't take responsibility until after the 1870s. After all the Indian Wars, they had to do something. And Virginians with Native American blood were denied official status by the federal government. Since the seventeenth century, many Virginia Indians had intermarried with European descendants. Every Sessoms I know has blue eyes, bright blue eyes like Hester. Anyway, this gets the feds out of any form of repayment or protections as near as I can tell."

"That doesn't let the Commonwealth off the hook," Cooper shrewdly said.

"Doesn't." Harry returned to the murder. "Well, you know a bit more than yesterday."

"Just enough to make this more confusing." Cooper suddenly smiled. "But you know, sooner or later, a picture emerges. You get a feeling. For all the legwork in the world, for all the computer checks and cross-checks, I still rely on that hunch. It will come."

"Maybe it has something to do with fish. A two-thousand-dollar fly rod."

"Harry, you can be really awful."

"I know."

"*So true!*" Pewter sat up to give her remark emphasis.

8

*T*hat same evening, glittering stars pierced the night. Looking out the tall, high windows of the old schoolhouse, Hester Martin could vaguely make out the obelisk in the cemetery a mile down the tertiary state road. Occasionally a truck would pass. She thought she heard a coyote.

Sitting down at one of the small school desks, she took out her Moleskine notebook, flipped it open, pulled out a pen. Before she could write down her thoughts, a car pulled up outside, its headlights illuminating the windows, then both the motor and the lights turned off.

Within seconds, Tazio entered the lovely room accompanied by her yellow Labrador retriever, the popular Brinkley.

"Good to see you," said Hester. "I know you're busy, what with your job and various committees."

"Hester, I always have time for you and it's important we run through the Halloween Hayride." Tazio sat in the desk across the aisle from Hester's.

The desks remained in rows just as they were in 1965, when the school was abandoned.

"Gets dark so early now," Hester remarked. "Somehow it always affects me. Makes me sleepy." She laughed at herself.

"Makes me fat." Tazio ruefully smiled. "I always put on weight in the winter. This year I am determined not to do it."

"Natural. It's a natural cycle."

"You never gain weight. Neither does Harry," Tazio said.

"With me it's high metabolism. That or worry. As to Harry, both her mother and father stayed slim. They worked hard, those people. So does Harry and so do you."

"Hard enough, but most of the time I'm sitting on my butt. If I go to a building site or walk through construction, that's about it. I need to join a gym."

"You look just fine. I wanted you to see these buildings from the inside. This one, the middle one, was literally the middle school. Has some lab equipment, not much. Everything these students got was already used, passed down. The books especially were worn." She thought a moment. "Your outstanding work for the library is almost done. We still have to raise money but your architectural work is complete and so practical. That's why I wanted you to see this."

"Funny, I've driven by these schoolhouses from time to time but never stopped. I always wanted to."

"They're built to last." She pointed to the windows. "So much natural light saved lighting money. When my mother was small, each of these buildings had a wood-burning stove smack in the middle. You can't see the hole for the flue, as when the stoves were removed the workmen patched the ceiling. Put in oil-fired heat. And since the county still pays the electric bill and fills up those old tanks, there is low heat here throughout the cold weather. The pipes don't freeze."

Tazio rose, walked to the back of the room, with Brinkley following her, and opened a door. "Well, they put a bathroom in, too."

"Right around the time of World War One. That's what my

mother said." Hester smiled, pulling an old-fashioned long key from her coat pocket, a grosgrain ribbon attached. "Come here."

Tazio and Brinkley walked back. "Wow, that's really old."

"Hold out your hand," Hester ordered, dropping the key into the young woman's outstretched palm. "This key opens all the doors. It's the master key. I've had it for years." She held up her hand. "Long story made short: I took it back in the eighties. Didn't trust the county commissioners or anyone else, really. Tazio, consider bringing these buildings back to life. Oh, it will take time, money, and lots of political organizing, but you of all people can imagine the possibilities if we saved the buildings' best features. No lowered ceilings."

Tazio looked around. "For what purpose? It won't be used as a school again."

"I don't know about that. It's possible it could be the basis for a small private school or a museum. You'll have to fight for it."

"And you are assigning me this task?" Tazio asked, eyebrows raised. "Aren't you going to help?"

"Yes, but"—she smiled weakly—"my brother died six years ago. Sometimes I think I'm not long for this world."

"Hester, I hope not." Tazio's voice registered concern.

Hester waved her hand. "No one knows, do they? I could live to one hundred or be gone tomorrow. Now come along with me. Bring the doggy."

"*Thank you,*" Brinkley replied.

The three of them piled into Hester's SUV. "Let me just review with you, briefly, the Halloween Hayride. I'll be in wagon one. You're the ringmaster. You've got to make sure our actors are in costume, go to their proper places. If anything is amiss, you fix it. I'm going to sit in hay and enjoy the show." She grinned.

Driving slowly, Hester headed north on the winding road, Buddy's cornfields on her left behind and around the schoolhouses.

She turned to Tazio in the passenger seat and said, "Okay, Frankenstein and Dr. Frankenstein will be in the schoolhouse. Goblins and ghosts that fly around will be in the dried-out cornfields. That ought to be scary, hearing the rustle."

"And it will be dark, too," said Tazio. "I checked my calendar. It's a couple of days after the new moon."

"As you know, the ghosts and goblins will be lit from within. Oh, this ought to scare the devil out of people." Hester stopped between two huge trees on each side of the road. "Jeepers Creepers will fly between the trees."

"Right." Tazio knew the order of events, but riding with Hester through the outdoor fright stations amplified how dramatic this year's hayride would be.

"We've got a cable to run between the trees. For the Headless Horseman—but you know him. Your boyfriend."

"Well, yes," Tazio laughed.

"Now, here's a good one." The middle-aged lady stopped on the road, the stone retaining wall of the graveyard standing out against the night sky. "Jason with his chain saw battles Count Dracula. Don't forget to make a convincing arm to come out of a grave."

"Already have it. We aren't using a real grave. I imagine the family would be upset."

"Mmm." Hester cast her eyes toward the obelisk and a few other tall statues. "The big monuments—families had big money back then, and you know, every one of them came to wrack and ruin. The names still fill the county voting registers but not much else. Ever notice how sometimes money makes people stupid?"

Tazio laughed again. "Among other things. But if things are too easy, I guess people lose their ambition."

"Oh, the Villions, the Huntleys, the Yosts, they either gambled it away, drank it away, or made really bad business decisions."

"Wine, women, and song?" Tazio raised one eyebrow.

"I will give those families some credit. The women were beautiful, all married well. It was the men who went to hell in a handbasket. Well, anyway, on the other side of the graveyard you repel Dracula with a cross, and then just past you, Reverend Jones will be a monk with an electric torch guiding people to Mount Carmel Church. You can just see the little spire. Mount Carmel only has but so much money." She stopped. "We are paying them well for the use of the rec hall. Always a good idea to keep on the sunny side of any church." She stopped talking, turned the truck down the farm road on the north side of the graveyard, backed out to return to the schoolhouses.

"Aren't there something like twenty-two thousand Christian sects, each with different ideas?" Tazio asked.

"I don't know. I'm Catholic myself. Sometimes I believe it. Sometimes I don't. Mostly I love mass. But out here looking at the stars, that's my true church," Hester replied with great feeling.

"It's mine," Brinkley piped up.

"I know what you mean," Tazio quietly agreed.

"Where'd you put the key?"

"In my pants pocket. It's deeper than my coat's."

"Don't you lose that key. That's the master."

"No, ma'am, I won't."

"Good girl to call me ma'am. You always call a lady older than yourself ma'am."

Tazio laughed again. "Hester, we do that in St. Louis, too."

"Miss it?"

"Not really. I go home to see Mom and Dad but I don't think I could live in a big city anymore."

"Millions upon millions do." She pulled in to the parking lot, a flat dirt place, next to Tazio's car. "That's another thing that scares me: How can the newcomers appreciate these buildings? They move down here to escape the city, but they bring their ways and they want efficiency, services, bottom-line kind of thinking. Spending money on these historic buildings would seem stupid to them."

"Maybe not," said Tazio, taking the bait. "It's part of our history. No matter where you come from."

"Well." Hester slowed her speech. "I hope you're right. My true dream is that eventually we can buy these from the county. Ha!" She clapped her hands. "Won't that be a fight! Will it help that you're mixed race? Yes. Politically it will help. You have such wonderful gifts, gifts few people possess. You could bring these buildings back to life. Wouldn't it be glorious to hear laughter inside them?"

"Yes, it would," Tazio agreed.

Hester cut the motor, turned to face her. "I know people think I'm weird."

Tazio didn't quite know what to say. "You're different from most Virginia ladies."

"I speak my mind. I don't have the time for the minuet of politeness. Bores me."

"I certainly understand that." Tazio smiled, remembering what a jolt it was to move from Missouri to Virginia.

"Maybe I am weird. I get worked up about things, history, getting books into childrens' hands, bringing buildings back to life, righting old wrongs." She inhaled deeply. "I get ideas like everyone worries about carbon emissions. What about the billions of people breathing out CO_2? That has to damage the environment. I blurt out this stuff and then people think I'm weird. They don't want to think. That's the problem."

"It's painful to think, Hester."

Hester stared at her. "But you do."

"Only after I've exhausted every other alternative."

This made Hester giggle. "Sometimes I do that, too. Well, girl, I railroaded you into designing parts of the Crozet Library and now I'm railroading you again."

"You are," Tazio said honestly.

"Will you take this on?"

"You know I will. But you have to work with me."

"I will, Taz, but things can happen. If something happens to me, you carry the ball, hear?"

"Don't say that, Hester." She breathed deeply. "But if anything happens to you, I will carry the ball and vice versa."

"Deal," Hester quickly answered.

When Tazio and Brinkley drove away, Hester returned to the middle schoolhouse. Inside, she sat down, took out her notebook, and started to write, then paused. She walked up to the teacher's desk in the front of the room, pulled open a drawer, took out a yellowed square of paper, and wrote a name on it with her fountain pen. She'd just dropped a lot on Tazio. She knew that when the younger woman read this, her natural curiosity would do the rest. She returned it to the middle drawer, turned out the lights, and shut the door and locked it, for she had a backup key to the outside door. Hearing the satisfying click, she walked to her truck, then stopped a moment to study the stars. They'd been up there long before she was born and they'd be there long after she was gone. She found that comforting.

Tazio, driving home with Brinkley next to her, wrestled with emotion. Hester had touched her. She had a strong feeling that Hester must have a premonition of her death, and that the kindhearted eccentric was passing the torch on to her.

9

*T*ucker, left behind, mournfully watched as Susan Tucker, Harry's best friend, picked her up at six in the evening on Wednesday, October 16. Rushing from the house, Harry jumped into the Audi station wagon's passenger seat. Joined at the hip, friends since cradle days, these two discussed everything and everybody with each other daily. Of course, Harry had already told Susan about the scarecrow down at Farmville.

And Susan, naturally, had commanded her friend to stay out of it.

"Thanks for picking me up," said Harry, closing the door to the station wagon. They almost always rode together to the St. Luke's vestry meeting.

"Gives us more time. Anyway, I'm not sure I trust you by yourself." Susan smiled.

"You never make a mistake."

"Finally you've realized that." Susan reached the state road at the end of the long gravel drive, looking both ways. "Uh-oh, here comes Aunt Tally. Let's give her a wide berth."

The almost-101-year-old indomitable woman behind the wheel of her old Bronco beeped and waved, swerving slightly to the right but correcting herself, much to the gratitude, no doubt, of her passenger, her great-niece, Little Mim.

"Wonder where those two are going," said Harry. "This has got to be the first time Little Mim has left the baby."

"She's a new mother. He's only three months old. It's good she's left him with Blair."

"He's a good father. Bet Big Mim is there."

"Harry, you got that right. The new grandmother—wait, the only grandmother in the world—doesn't believe men can take care of babies. Well, in her defense, she said her husband never changed a diaper."

"They didn't back then." Harry knew that prior generations led more gender-defined lives.

"Plenty don't now, but in the main I think young men want to be involved. I remember my father at the end crying that he barely knew his children until he retired. Poor Dad. He did what men did. He worked his ass off and came home after we were asleep."

"Your father did work hard. He ran that lumberyard, and when you own the business, it owns you."

"You were lucky that you could farm with your father," Susan said without envy.

"I was. Mom was the librarian, so she would come home a little after I got home from school. We didn't have much money but we had a lot of love. My parents taught me a lot." She looked at Mount Tabor Presbyterian Church as they passed. "They taught me not to be a Presbyterian."

"Harry!"

Harry laughed. "Mom and Dad were generally open-minded people, but they did have their share of religious prejudice. If there had been a Church of England here, that's where they would have worshipped."

"Reminds me. You have your building-and-grounds notes for the vestry meeting?"

"Yeah. Why?"

"Because if there's ever an outlay of expenses, that's where it is," Susan said as she, too, eyed the lovely white Mount Tabor Church.

There was a bit of traffic on the narrow two-lane highway. People were driving home from work. In the morning and the evening, going could be slow.

"I never noticed that," Susan said, her voice rising.

"What? Mount Tabor is Mount Tabor. Really pretty."

"No. There's a Halloween scene on the grounds nearest the road."

Twisting to look back, sure enough, Harry saw pumpkins, tied-up cornstalks, baskets of harvest, and a jolly-looking witch on a broomstick over a sickle moon. Actually, the broomstick used the midpoint of the moon for stability.

"So?" Harry shrugged.

"Harry, pagan. Halloween is a pagan festival."

"It might have started that way," Harry said, "but then, Christmas is a co-opted pagan festival. So this became All Hallows' Eve and the early church fathers could sleep soundly at night."

Susan, who knew her history, maintained, "Pagan. When have you ever seen a church with a Halloween display?"

Harry shrugged. "I give Mount Tabor credit. It's fun."

"Yeah, I guess it is."

"Here we are," said Harry as Susan pulled the Audi into the Lutheran church's parking lot. "No Halloween display at St. Luke's. Leaves are raked. Grounds are sleek. Am I doing a good job or what?"

"Divine, darling."

"Well, it is our church."

The meeting took place in a twenty-by-thirty-foot room with a high ceiling. Built of native stone in the eighteenth century, St. Luke's emitted a feeling of peace, of thoughtfulness. And being Lutheran, it excelled in good works.

The Very Reverend Herbert C. Jones, a Vietnam veteran, deeply believed anyone could talk about Christ. One had to comfort one's fellow man. And he did, personally. His congregants did, too. St. Luke's provided tutoring for children in need. Also, their small soup kitchen had recently grown with the depression.

The Reverend Jones used innovative techniques to draw in his flock. Every October 4th, on St. Francis's Day, people brought their animals to the church for a blessing. This year's service had proved especially unusual in that a young woman brought a jar of worms. She had started a worm farm and wanted the reverend's blessing. The clergyman dutifully picked up the jar and blessed those worms as though they had been devoted dogs. We are all God's creatures.

When reprimanded by a parishioner for keeping a saint's day—"leave that to the Catholics"—Herb took no offense. He merely replied that the saints were as good a model for Lutherans as they were for Catholics. And who could be a better example for all than St. Francis of Assisi?

The St. Luke's vestry board, six people, usually met the second Wednesday of each month.

Elocution, Cazenovia, and Lucy Fur, the Lutheran cats, invariably joined the proceedings.

These meetings generally ran smoothly until the group had to consider expenditures. Last year, the old church truck breathed its last. The unplanned expense of a new four-wheel-drive truck had sent the church treasurer, Neil Jordan, into a tailspin. Now in his second year on the board, Neil wanted to impress his fellow parishioners as a fiscal conservative. He was always seeking new ways to save money. But also, he was beginning to discover if it wasn't one thing, it was another, and the bills piled up.

Neil read the treasurer's report. He looked straight at Harry over his tortoiseshell glasses, expensive ones from Ben Silver in Charleston. "You're the one I worry about."

BoomBoom Craycroft, another childhood friend of Harry's as well as Susan's, laughed a little, as did the reverend.

"Neil, all the church's equipment is in good order," Harry assured him. "We can get one more year out of the leaf blower, and I fixed the zero-turn mower this summer. We're in good shape except for one small necessity."

Neil froze. "Yes?"

"There's a small portion of the slate roof right on that northwest corner which gets hit the hardest," said Harry. "Two of the shingles have dislodged, and with one more hard blow, I'm afraid we will lose a larger section than need be. I climbed up there."

"Harry, I wish you wouldn't do that," Reverend Jones admonished her.

"Rev, I'm in charge of buildings and grounds."

The good pastor said, "Surely there's a man who can do some of this."

"Are we going to have the Sexism 101 talk?" BoomBoom laughed. "We are supposed to be long past that caveman talk, Rev."

"No, but . . ." The Reverend Jones sighed heavily.

Looking at the beloved clergyman, Harry compromised. "How about next time I go up on the roof, I take someone with me, possibly someone male who is actually a roofer? I can do it but we need a professional up there."

This truly alarmed Neil. "Roofing costs an arm and a leg!"

Keeping her tone level, Harry replied, "It does. However, if we don't attend to this right now before the weather turns—and you know how bad the winds get in winter straight through March—we will most certainly lose more slate shingles. The water will run into the beams and travel from there. I doubt it will come through the ceiling, though, unless a huge hole is blown into the roof. We'd need a big tree limb to accomplish that—I think. But that sort of silent water damage will come back to haunt us, years from now when the building's wood beams rot out. Pay now or pay later, big-time."

The members of the vestry board were persuaded, as was the reverend.

Neil, defeated, asked, "Do you have a ballpark figure?"

"That's why I would like to get a professional roofer up there. My personal guess is if we do this now, we can do it for about thirty-five hundred dollars."

"Thirty-five hundred! For two shingles?" Neil's voice cracked.

"No. I estimate we will need to replace about a two-foot square. True slate shingles are expensive, plus we have to try and match shingles that are over two hundred and forty years old. The labor is expensive, too, but once we have the materials, it's not an all-day job. Oh, and I expect there will be a gas surcharge if the gas prices go up again."

"That's the truth. Everyone's doing it." BoomBoom, her beautiful mane of blonde hair catching the light, nodded. "There's no way business, small business, can absorb those prices and still make a profit."

"How about the post office?" asked Harry, the former postmistress. "I can't even imagine what a one-cent increase in gasoline does to their budget. Delivery trucks, cars in every state in this nation—it has to be mind-boggling."

Wesley Speer shook his head. Also new to the board, he owned a high-end realty firm. They'd felt the downturn but not nearly as badly as Realtors in Las Vegas or other large cities. Wesley believed once the foreclosure mess cleared up, maybe in another two years, the economy might pick up some momentum. He knew he'd never again see the craziness, the flipping of houses and farms, that he saw in, say, 2007, but he was confident sales would rebound. If people can get work, they want to own a home. He'd built a life's career on that.

Susan joined the conversation. "Did you read in the paper where our area, Richmond in particular, has the worst postal service in the country?"

"Your husband's in the House of Delegates," Neil teased her. "Make him fix it."

"Virginia's state government can't fix the federal postal system, but you know Ned would if he could. I swear that man is a glutton for punishment. He actually loves being in the House of Delegates." Susan threw her hands up in the air.

"He must be a glutton for punishment, he married you." Harry smiled so sweetly.

"Well, I think this meeting is over, unless there's more discussion concerning the roof," the Reverend Jones said, enjoying the banter between the two old friends.

The committee members zoomed toward the kitchen, some heading straight for the bar. The vestry board enjoyed getting together after the meeting, catching up on one another's news and listening to Reverend Jones, who had an appropriate Bible quote at the ready for just about any topic of conversation.

Lucy Fur wove between people's legs. *"Do drop something, will you?"* the cat urged the thoughtless humans munching away on ham biscuits.

Elocution, the senior cat, curled up in Reverend Jones's lap.

Cazenovia picked out Susan for her victim. Susan couldn't take a step without Cazenovia sticking right next to her, meowing.

"Suffer the little kitties to come unto you," the reverend joked.

Libations in hand, all sat in chairs around the coffee table, books pushed to the middle.

"Harry," Wesley said, "you've known Buddy Janss longer than I have. Why won't he sell the one hundred acres behind the old abandoned schoolhouses? Be very profitable for him."

"More to the point," BoomBoom interjected, "why doesn't the county finally do something about those schoolhouses? Old well-built buildings can still be useful. Instead, the county blows millions on new construction. Everything has to be new."

"Plans for repairs tend to languish in the county budget." Reverend Jones's deep voice rumbled. "But it's much as you say, BoomBoom, everything has to be new and, to my way of thinking, antiseptic. Those three wooden buildings, with their big tall windows, beckon one to learn." He smiled. "Can't you imagine sitting at one of the old desks with the flip-top lid we all used, staring out the windows on an early spring day? If nothing else, might make you want to learn about the environment."

The group laughed.

Harry answered Wesley's question as best she could: "Buddy fears development, and for good reason. The school buildings and those acres are in a prime spot."

Wesley tried not to sound too judgmental, even though he was. "He would make so much money. At least three point two million. These are hard times. That profit would allow him to buy or rent much more land farther west in the county or he could invest it in bonds or something."

"Buddy isn't averse to profit, but like I said, he fears development," said Harry. "He thinks good soil, good farmland, should stay farmland. Wesley, he isn't going to sell."

"Mmm." Wesley heard Harry's words but he still hoped he could find a way to pry those one hundred acres from Buddy.

"Don't forget, Wesley, the schoolhouses could create a problem for any development." Susan Tucker kicked off her shoes. "Sorry, my feet hurt."

"Yeah, you guys should be forced to wear heels just once in your life," Harry said. "Torture," she declared, grinning.

"Well, these are low heels but I've had enough." Susan rubbed her right foot. "Okay, the problem: County land remains county land. And those school buildings might be considered historically significant. Now, the county can elect to sell its land. There must be a public hearing advertised in the newspaper each week for a month. These days the announcement has to go on the county website, too."

Neil spoke up. "You think the fear is that if the one hundred acres go, whoever purchases same will have no use for the schoolhouses and demolish them. That's jumping the gun, I'd say."

Harry's mouth fell open a little, then she said, "I hadn't thought that far ahead, but I guess it could be a real concern."

"Those schoolhouses would make welcome living quarters for the aged," said BoomBoom, thinking out loud. "Nice setting, pretty grounds, easy access from the state road and not really far from Route 250."

"Or condominiums, which would bring the county more revenue than what we used to call the poorhouse." Reverend Jones drained his glass.

"What do you mean?" Harry, one of the younger people in the room, asked him.

The reverend clarified, "Honey, back when the earth was cooling, every county in this state had its own poorhouse, and it was usually a farm. Those down on their luck worked the farm. We don't have that anymore, but a place for the aged is somewhat like that in that anyone dependent on government-subsidized living is usually poor. 'Course, at Random Row, they wouldn't have to do farm work."

"Random Row?" BoomBoom repeated. "I remember Mother saying that once or twice, but I figured she was just forgetting the actual name of the place."

"It's a great name," Neil said, nodding to Reverend Jones. "Be a great name for condominiums."

"'Tis, but I doubt they would be called that," Reverend Jones quickly replied.

"All right, Rev, what's the story?" Harry plied him.

"Well," he said, "those schoolhouses were built for the African American children. When I was little, you didn't use terms like 'African American.' The polite word was 'colored'—polite among white folks, anyway. Really, back then no one said things like 'Italian American' either. Well, I'm getting off the track, but I do think about these things sometimes. Anyway, so many of the children at the schoolhouses had white fathers. Rarely did the men visit the school, because often they were married to white women, but many of those men did support their children, the random children, economically."

A silence followed this, then Susan said, "Nothing is simple, is it?"

"Not when it comes to human beings." Reverend Jones smiled. "What always strikes me is how most of us try to normalize an abnormal situation. I guess I learned this in Vietnam. We just struggled to keep things tied down. I mean, all I could think about apart from staying alive was, how were the Baltimore Orioles doing? We'd all try to get baseball scores and then football scores. If my team lost and one of my buddies gloated, fistfight. Here we were in a war in a different world, and we'd fight over a football score. But it felt safe in a way. Random Row was kind of the same thing, people normalizing a difficult situation."

"The desegregation act was enforced in 1965," Susan informed them. "That resolved it."

"You weren't born yet." Reverend Jones smiled at her. "It resolved political issues; it did not nor could not resolve personal issues. If your father is white and doesn't claim you, you may not be thinking about desegregation the same way."

Neil looked at the reverend. "What's the old saying, 'The personal is political'?"

"Is and isn't." BoomBoom was firm about this. "But in 1965, what happened to these so-called random kids' schools?"

"Abandoned," said Reverend Jones. "It was a political victory but it came at an unintended price. At least, I think it did. Basically, the children from Random Row were crammed into the white schools with no support system. The assumption was and still is that white ways are better. I don't exactly see this as black and white, I see it more in class terms, but the reality of the children at Random Row was most of them were African American or mixed race, and poor. They were thrown into schools with children from a higher socioeconomic group and with vastly different needs. Not a good thing, in my mind."

"Well, it's a done deal," Wesley replied with no emotion.

"It is." The reverend nodded. "But that doesn't mean we can't learn from it, and not repeat our mistakes. We have to think of people's emotions."

"What happened to the teachers at Random Row?" asked Boom-Boom; at forty-one, she was the same age as Harry and Susan.

"I suspect they were bought off. You know, early retirement or something like that. I guess what really gets my blood up is the assumption those teachers weren't as well educated. Howard? Grambling? The list of excellent black colleges can go on. The teachers may have gone to segregated colleges, but tell you what, I never met any graduate of those colleges who wasn't well educated."

"Racism is subtle and not so subtle." Susan grabbed a cookie from the plate that Reverend Jones had placed on the table.

"So is sexism," said BoomBoom.

"Yes, but you ladies have so many ways to even the score," Neil teased her.

"Don't forget that, Neil," BoomBoom teased him right back.

"Not to ignore this fascinating history," interjected Wesley, "but what I deduce from this is that the county, which could realize high profits on those buildings, won't for political reasons?"

"Don't you think it depends on the budget?" said Harry. "We're in hard times. If the Board of County Commissioners wants to let those buildings and the land go, this would be the time."

"If they're willing to put up with the protest that our history is being demolished," said Neil, in between bites of a chocolate chip cookie. "Here's what I think. Use them or sell them. To keep the land idle, just sitting there, is stupid."

"Do you think Buddy would sell his hundred acres to the county?" Wesley asked.

"They wouldn't need it," Harry replied.

"Probably not," said Wesley. "I mean, if a housing development was part of the plan, yes. Otherwise, no. It does seem wasteful, though. The schoolhouses just abandoned and going to ruin."

Susan simply said, "I say restore the buildings as a museum. It could be a good lesson for all and those rooms have cozy, lovely proportions. I'm like Reverend Jones, everything today is too antiseptic and big. I'm really tired of big."

———

After an hour of lively talk, the group began to trickle out. Harry, Susan, and BoomBoom stayed longest, helping Herb clean up, washing dishes and glasses.

Drying her hands, BoomBoom remarked to Harry, "I was so sorry to hear that Big Mim lost the Medaglia d'Oro filly. Stunning, that filly."

"Fair was devastated. He thought she was one of the most perfectly formed horses he had ever seen. Big Mim was, well, in tears according to Fair, but still took it like a trooper. Being a grandmother was a comfort, I think."

"Heard she doesn't like the boy's name, Roland."

"Little Mim and Blair love the ancient history of Roland at the Roncevaux Pass. 'Course, Big Mim just ignored it and calls him Roy."

BoomBoom laughed. "Those two never have gotten along. Still, they do love each other."

"Would you want to be Big Mim's daughter?" asked Harry.

"No," the blonde replied. "I love being her friend, though."

"Me, too. She's one hell of a horsewoman."

They nattered on, Susan chiming in as she wiped down the coffee table, Herb as he put away glasses. Each lady kissed Herb's cheek, then each other as they left St. Luke's.

On the drive home, the stars glittered in pale silver light. Friday would be a full moon.

"Good meeting." Susan hit her brights. "At least Neil isn't talking about algorithms anymore. He gave a straightforward treasurer's report."

"He's figuring out that simple is better," Harry said. "Always is, too, no matter what the subject."

"Ned says what drives him crazy about his fellow politicians in Richmond is how they complicate things to make themselves look smarter. He also said the level of discourse is so low a man of average intelligence has to stoop to match it." She smiled. "But there are some good people there in both chambers. He likes working with David Toscano and he likes working with some of the people from the farming counties. He's not too thrilled with the ones from northern Virginia."

"Like I said before, he's a glutton for punishment."

They rounded the curve, Mount Tabor up ahead.

"My tire light went on. Reach into the glove compartment and get out my pressure check, will you?" Susan turned in to Mount Tabor's parking lot. "Oh, dear, Witchy Woo has fallen over. Come on, let's set her up. They put a lot of work into this. Then I'll check my tire."

The two kept the brights on in the direction of the display and walked over.

They reached the corn bundles, all the arranged pumpkins, some cut as jack-o'-lanterns, the large baskets overflowing with gourds and squashes. Witchy Woo had fallen uphill onto the uneven ground.

Harry sniffed. "Something's gone off."

Susan inhaled. "Just. Probably a dead gopher somewhere. He'll be gone tomorrow."

Harry bent over to pick up the tumbled-over figure, noticing that its rubber mask was complete with a long, warty witch's nose. She stood up again. "It's not a gopher."

Both women stared at the black-clad figure.

"Good God." Susan put her hand to her face.

Harry reached down to pull off the mask.

Susan shouted, grabbing her arm, "Don't!"

10

"*A*ren't you off work tonight?" Harry, still upset, asked as Cooper crossed the parking lot in her civilian clothing.

"I am, but Dabny called me from headquarters and said that you, once again, have found a strange corpse. So here I am. Anyway, I'd like to see this before the body goes to the state medical examiner. You two stay here. I *mean* it."

"All right," Susan firmly agreed. "I'll take charge of Harry."

Cooper turned her back to walk away, then faced them again. "Are you two doing okay?"

Harry shrugged, and fibbed a tad. "Yeah. It's gross but . . ." She shrugged again as Susan nodded in assent.

The police investigative team circled the display. The photographer snapped, stepping out of the way of the officers.

Dorothy Maddox, chief of forensics, had only been with the team a year. She was kneeling down, surgical gloves on, carefully touching the corpse's arm. In the temporary lights now shining on the scene, she studied a swollen hand, and a forearm with purple splotches.

Cooper stood behind Dorothy. "Thirty-six hours at most, my guess."

"Your guess isn't far wrong. The nights have been cold, the days in the seventies. She's on the other side of maximum rigor mortis, obviously, but intact, and that's a huge help." Dorothy stood up. "Is Rick on the way?"

No sooner was his name spoken than the sheriff pulled off the road and into the church driveway. He, too, was in his civilian clothes and driving his personal vehicle. He glanced toward Harry, then walked over to the scene.

"We'll need to dust everything. The pumpkins, the baskets, every single thing." He took a deep breath, then coughed slightly. "I hated to leave my ball game, but this is, well, original." He paused. "There's nothing like the odor of death, is there? It isn't even that bad yet. I'm surprised the body wasn't damaged."

"Boss, can I remove the victim's mask?" Dorothy asked. "I waited for you."

"Yes, of course." Rick motioned for all the lights to shine on the witch's face.

Carefully, Dorothy removed the rubber mask with the hooked nose.

"My God," Susan exclaimed, as she could see the face with the flashlight focused on it. "It's Hester Martin!"

Harry recognized her all the way from where she stood in the parking lot. She covered her mouth with her hand, then let it fall. "Hester Martin. She never did a thing to anybody."

Tears filled Susan's eyes for the middle-aged lady. Her mind flashed to Hester proudly showing off produce, filling her specially decorated wooden wheelbarrows, some worn and painted green, some barn red, some faded marine blue. Large wheels were yellow with a pinstripe matching the color of the painted display cart. Hester had a good eye for proportion and color. The produce gleamed, as she had misted it, too. Susan's tears rolled faster now. She met Harry's eyes. "Remember when Hester declared that black gum trees were conspiring against humans? Well, everyone gets a free pass for a few crackbrained ideas. Hester's seemed more imaginative than most."

"I can't believe this!" exclaimed Harry. She, too, cried a bit.

Rick was as surprised as they at the victim's identity. "Dorothy, get the body out of here as soon as you can. We're lucky it's night."

"Sure. I've done what I can do without disturbing the rest of this Halloween scene."

"Here's Ted. Excuse me."

Rev. Ted Foster had driven over as soon as the sheriff's office called him. He lived about twenty minutes up Route 810. Along the way, he'd had the presence of mind to pick up Bunky Fouche, the church groundskeeper.

Seeing Hester laid out in the witchy garb, Bunky had to be steadied.

Rick escorted both men directly to the corpse.

Bunky shook uncontrollably. "Oh, Sheriff, I can't look at dead bodies."

"Bunky, tell me who this is."

"It's Hester Martin, God rest her sweet soul. She was good to me."

"Reverend Foster." Rick turned to the minister, who also appeared shaken by the grisly sight and rank odor. "When did you put up this Halloween crèche, for lack of a better word?"

"Three days ago," answered Reverend Foster, his voice low. "The witch was a manikin and she had straw hair."

"And did you look at the display each day?"

"No, sir, I didn't. From a distance, it all looked fine to me."

"It was fine." Bunky's voice quavered.

"So, neither of you has any idea when Hester Martin's body was placed here?" Frustration edged into the sheriff's tone.

"No," both answered.

Rick put his hand under Bunky's elbow to steady him, walking him away from the eerie but all-too-real vision.

Cooper watched the men's departure, then said to Dorothy, "It's a lot of work to carry a body, dress it up, place it on the broom."

Harry had inched closer from the parking lot, and piped up. "Maybe Hester's body was already dressed up when it was brought here. The killer first observed the manikin's witch outfit and dressed her just the same. I mean, it makes sense the killer would make it easy on himself."

Cooper stared at Harry, thought a moment, then replied, "A possibility."

Susan said, "If Hester's body had been here for any real length of time, dogs would have already gotten at it, crows, flies. We're all country people. We know the stages of death."

The three women stood silent.

"We've got a real sicko," Cooper replied simply, saying what they were all thinking: The killer had kept Hester's body somewhere else and placed it here once rigor mortis decreased and the muscles relaxed.

"Coop, let me get poor Hester out of here." Dorothy motioned for the stretcher and the body bag. "I need to get her in the cooler at the morgue before there's more damage. And maybe when I get the costume off, I'll know how she was murdered."

"If the modus operandi is the same as our scarecrow accountant, we've got a major problem," said Coop.

Dorothy whispered, "No matter what, we've got a major problem."

11

*F*air ran out to the drive at 11:10 P.M., when his wife finally drove up with Susan.

"Why didn't you let me come to you?" Harry's husband asked, his voice betraying his concern.

Harry opened the door to get out as Susan rolled down the window. The dog and the two cats also ran out of the house at Harry's arrival.

"Honey, there was enough confusion," she said. "Susan and I were together. We're all right."

"We are," Susan reassured Fair. "I mean, as all right as you can be after finding something like that." She took a deep breath. "Let me get on home. My dog needs to go to the bathroom."

"Where's Ned?" Fair asked.

"In Richmond."

"Why don't you stay here?" he invited her.

"I appreciate that but Owen needs to go out and I'll feel better with him, at home, with a hot bath and bed."

"Sure?" he asked, his eyebrows raised.

"Sure. And when I get there, if I can't do as well as I think I can, I'll bring Owen back with me and we'll bunk up with you all."

"Okay," he agreed.

Harry leaned in the window, gave Susan a kiss. "I'll call you tomorrow."

"Better." Susan rolled up the window and turned the car around. Her two friends and their animal companions watched her motor down the long drive.

Slipping his arm around her waist, Fair walked Harry back into the house.

"*Must be good,*" Pewter said, meaning another big mess Harry had stumbled into.

"*If only we could have heard the phone call,*" Mrs. Murphy said.

"*Yeah. I hate not knowing.*" Tucker followed right on Harry's heels, resisting the urge to slightly bite them.

Once inside, closing the kitchen door against the chill, Harry surprised Fair as she sat at the table. "I'd like a drink. What should I have?"

"Oh, how about if I make you a simple scotch and soda? Not too strong."

"You know I can't drink. But I need something," she said, stating the obvious.

"This will relax you and help you sleep. No nightmares." He opened the pie safe, where the liquor bottles were lined up like orderly soldiers.

Neither husband nor wife was much of a drinker, but there were spirits on hand for guests. Fair occasionally liked a cold beer at night in the summer and a scotch in the winter, but he could go days without a drink.

Tucker lifted her head. "*Scotch has an interesting smell. Not bad.*"

"*Tuna is better,*" Pewter remarked, patrolling the kitchen counter.

"*Can't drink tuna.*" Mrs. Murphy jumped up on the corner.

Pushed by Fair, Harry took a sip of the scotch, then recounted everything. When she finished her tale, she sighed, then said, "Tell me about your day. I don't want to think about this anymore."

"I'm sorry, honey. I'm just worried and I want you to carry the old .38. Your father's Smith and Wesson is as good as the day it was made."

"Why? I'm in no danger."

"Probably not, but you found two bodies and it seems likely both were done in by the same killer or killers. You will be in the paper and on TV. A bad guy might wonder why Harry Haristeen has a nose for murder."

" 'Nose' is the right word." Harry wrinkled hers.

"Humans can't smell worth squat." Pewter leapt onto the counter with Mrs. Murphy.

"Even a human can smell a corpse that's been dead for a bit, the days being warm. It's not the full-blown effect but they can tell." With her phenomenal powers of smell, Tucker knew of what she spoke.

"Sometimes I wonder how they survive." Pewter looked out the window over the sink, where the last moth of the year fluttered.

Unaware of the animals' condescending observations, Fair leaned back in his chair. "Pretty easy day today, so I actually got a little research done. Stem cell stuff."

"Haven't you used stem cell therapies?"

"Not much, honey, though I'd like to. It's complicated but those treatments really work for horses' musculoskeletal injuries. Vets have been using stem cell transplants since 2005. The problem is that there are bogus firms on the Internet that claim stem cell therapies can treat laminitis and neurological conditions, and that's not true."

Harry knew that "laminitis" meant an inflammation of the sensitive tissue of a horse's hoof.

"I guess there are scam artists in every profession," she lamented.

"There are, but when they cause suffering to living creatures, my blood boils. Someone without veterinary knowledge or degree, but with every good intention in the world to help their horse, gets on the Internet, finds a bogus product, buys it, and their horse continues to suffer."

"Do you think the stem cell transplants used for horses will work for people?"

He folded his hands together. "Yes. But there again, as the science progresses, you will have doctors making wild claims or dishonest companies doing so."

Fair was such a fount of knowledge that sometimes Harry fired question after question at him. "You think in time the obstacles for using human stem cells will be removed?"

"In some cases they already have, and while I believe in relieving suffering, I have to think about this one. It truly is a complex moral issue."

"Maybe everything is, honey," Harry said.

"Yes. Take murder. It seems cut and dried, doesn't it? And yet surely there are times when murder is justified. A wife defends herself and her children against a rampaging husband. I couldn't find it in my heart to condemn such a woman. Throughout all of nature, mothers kill or die defending their young."

"Nothing is really that clear cut, is it?" Harry agreed.

"Well, the Ten Commandments make it seem so, but I guess there are exceptions to every rule, even those. Maybe that means I'm going to hell." He half-smiled.

"You're the best man I know," she said, smiling his way. "And there have to be millions of people who ask questions, who wonder. What helps me is talking to Reverend Jones. I don't know what I would do without him."

"I should talk to him about this." Fair unfolded his hands. "That and genetic engineering. We may be on the cusp of creating a super horse, and if we do that, people aren't far behind."

"That's a terrifying thought."

"It will start out safely enough. A tag on a gene sequence will be discovered to cause some kind of cancer. Doctors will get in there and manipulate the sequence. It sounds far-fetched but it isn't. Just look at the genetic manipulations you've seen in crops."

She took a long sip of scotch. "You know, when I was a kid, Dad and I would sit down with the seed catalogues. We'd try and figure out which corn could survive a drought, too much rain, which one had the sweetest taste. You had so many choices and now, well, you really don't. I look in my catalogues and there's just one page for corn, and every offering has disease resistance, a list of qualifications. Me, I just want Silver Queen," she said, citing an especially delicious corn usually available at central Virginia vegetable stands in August. Her eyes misted. "Hester sold the best Silver Queen."

"Brave new world." He smiled at her. "I am so sorry you found Hester. So sorry."

"If it's a brave new world, that means we have to be brave to face it. But I remember the Law of Unintended Consequences. You never know what you're stirring up."

"By God, that's the truth," he said, slipping his arm around her again.

"But these murders have very intended consequences. They were carefully planned and enacted, and inflicted on the rest of us. That means there's a message. You don't do something as elaborate as this unless it's an attempt to make a statement of some sort."

"And that's why you'd better carry your father's snubnose .38." Fair's voice was firm.

12

*F*riday the air sparkled, the leaves exploded with color, and the temperature hung at about forty-seven degrees. Fall ushered in many changes. Fur-covered animals now had their thick undercoat, the outer coat shining luxuriously. With the waning of daylight, chickens laid less eggs. All those creatures slowed down by summer's heat now surged with energy. Robins and some ducks and geese had already departed on their southern journey, as had the monarch butterflies. Everyone else busied themselves with nest repair. Turtles readied for sleep, along with other amphibians and reptiles. Toads lined their shallow nests with straw, hay, anything that could insulate, as did mice, who could unravel a sweater quickly.

Harry had once left a thick wool sweater in the tack room only to come back the next morning to find mice had chewed big holes in it, all of that fine wool now lining their nests behind the wall. Those mice lived good.

This perfect October morning, having just finished the barn chores, Harry tossed up some jelly beans for the possum in the hayloft, then shook the hay bits out of her hair.

"*Don't shake that on me,*" complained a perfectly groomed Pewter, languishing below.

"All right, who's ready to go?" asked Harry.

"Me!" Tucker ran in from the back of the barn.

"Me, too," Mrs. Murphy echoed her friend.

Both eagerly sat in the center aisle as Harry hung up her big wide sweeper. "That's two. Let me check on Pewts."

"Leave her here," Tucker advised. "She's such a priss and a pain."

Pewter lifted her head from her paws. "I heard that."

She'd been sleeping in the tack room, disturbed only when Harry had shaken out the hay while looking in the big mirror.

"Come on," Harry urged her.

"I have nothing to wear," Pewter replied facetiously.

"Just leave her," Tucker practically begged.

Much as Pewter wished to languish in the tack room, the prospect of irritating the corgi held greater allure. She rose, stretching fore and aft, then daintily leapt to the floor and sauntered out the tack room door.

"Peon," the gray cat remarked to the sitting dog as she passed.

"Pissant," Tucker fired back.

Tucker flattened her ears and readied herself to lunge after the large cat, but Mrs. Murphy whispered, "Cool it."

"How can I let her get away with that?" asked Tucker.

"If you growl or chase after her, Mom will leave you here. She hates fights in the truck or car, you know that."

Tucker's ears drooped, her expression saddened. "That cat gets away with murder."

Pewter, full sashay working—a swing to the right, a swing to the left—called over her shoulder, "I am fascinating. Harry never likes to go anywhere without me. You, on the other hand, are a mere drooling dog. So eager to please. Peon. You really are a peon."

Mrs. Murphy walked tightly next to her canine friend. "Ignore her."

Harry opened the door to the 1978 Ford F-150, a half-ton

pickup truck you couldn't kill on Judgment Day. The two cats jumped onto the floorboard while the human bent over to pick up the solid dog. "Onf."

"*Don't call me fat.*" Pewter grinned as the dog was placed on the seat.

"*I'm a lot bigger than you,*" Tucker said, defending her weight.

"*Oh, la,*" the cat sang out, then crawled onto Harry's lap once she was behind the wheel.

Harry could easily drive with a cat in her lap, so she fired up the old engine, listened to the melodic deep rumble, then pulled around and down the long drive.

"*Where are we going?*" Pewter asked.

"Okay, you all, we're going to Crème de la Crème. I am finally going to break down and buy two of those heavy Italian mugs."

"*She understood?*" Tucker's ears shot up.

"*Of course she didn't,*" Pewter laughed. "*She just likes to hear herself yak.*"

"*Look who's talking,*" Tucker said in a low voice to Mrs. Murphy.

"*I have good ears, you know,*" Pewter said.

"*You do,*" Mrs. Murphy agreed.

"*It's your attitude that's not so good.*" Tucker had to say it.

The gray cat turned her back on the other two on the bench seat, rested her chin on Harry's left forearm, and watched the passing scenery out the side window.

Slowing for a turn, Harry could see the houses on the ridge at the Old Trail development. Below, she spotted Buddy Janss on his huge tractor, harvesting his soybeans. The other side of the road was filled with corn: some rows cut, others left standing to dry. On the road, yellow metal signs about the size of the old Burma Shave signs marked the rows. Each sign showed a golden ear of corn with two green leaves folded back. Below that, the seed company Demeter was identified in red letters, and under that in black Arabic numerals were the seed ID numbers. Buddy Janss had worked with Demeter for years and this was his test field. His other acres were dedicated to revenue crops.

Harry pulled off the road as Buddy cut the motor of his tractor. He climbed down to check something on the attachment. Satisfied, he turned to climb back up.

"Buddy!" Harry called out as she walked toward him, with three four-footed friends in tow.

"Harry." He smacked his baseball hat on his leg. "After hearing the news, I was going to call you, girl, but I figured you'd had enough."

He wrapped his massive arms around her, giving her a hug as she kissed his cheek.

"I appreciate that. It was crazy."

He put his hand on her shoulder. "I can't believe it, just can't believe it."

"Me neither."

"Now, Hester was peculiar, no doubt, but she was a good girl." He wiped a tear from his eye with his handkerchief.

"I've been racking my brain to think who could do such a thing."

"Can't think of a soul, can you? Who would want to hurt Hester?" He looked into her eyes. "She could get in your face about things, stuff she really cared about, like ethanol, but you don't kill someone over ethanol. And there were certain people she just wouldn't do business with, but how much money would a farmer lose by not having his produce sold at Hester's? I'm like you, racking my brain."

"I've been thinking over her many pet projects, pet peeves," said Harry. "We all know she loved the Crozet Library. She loved history and wanted to preserve as much of our history as she could. She also cared about farming practices." Harry laughed as the tears rolled down her face. "I don't think Hester ever saw an abandoned building she didn't want to save. Like some people save animals, she tried to save existing buildings or raise funds for a building the community needs. Remember when she was afraid the old Coca-Cola building would be torn down? And I think she checked into the three abandoned school buildings there by your one hundred acres. Oh, also she wanted to have designated as a historical spot the house where Georgia O'Keeffe lived ever so briefly. You don't murder someone over any of that." Harry cried more, which made Buddy join in.

Buddy, like most powerful men in this part of the world, readily showed emotion. Bighearted to a fault, they wanted to hold babies, pet your dogs, take your arm as though you needed guidance, and to help any lady, old, young, pretty or not.

Harry wiped her eyes, then reached up and wiped Buddy's. "I hate that someone made a mockery of her in her death," she said.

"You know, girl, sooner or later that S.O.B. will make a mistake, and I want to be there."

Little did Buddy or Harry know, he would get his wish.

13

*T*hat afternoon, Harry peered down at Mrs. Murphy, Pewter, and Tucker, all sitting at her feet in the tack room. "Remind me never to buy an Italian desk lamp again."

After two years, the high-intensity bulb had burned out. The lamp boasted appealingly sleek design, but getting its bulb out was proving infuriating. She had to flip back the head of the angular lamp, figure out how to remove the frosted-glass square, then dislodge the small cylindrical bulb.

A rustle of mice behind the tack box irritated Mrs. Murphy. She left her human and jumped on top of the box, squinting behind it. *"Stay put,"* she warned.

Martha, the savvy mother of many, giggled. *"We've never heard so much cussing in our lives."*

The tiger cat smiled. *"You know our bargain."*

"I do, but think of my children. Such language." Martha looked up into the predator's green eyes.

Years ago the two cats had made a deal with the mice who lived behind the baseboard in the tack room. The insulated tack room walls provided toasty winter lodging, along with the yarn, hay bits, and old rag pieces the mice brought in to further line their nests. So long as the mice didn't show themselves or chew tack or

saddle pads, they could eat whatever fell in the horses' stalls. This way the cats didn't look as though they'd fallen down on the job and the mice could tidy up the horses' mess. Also, mice heard things domestic animals did not. They occasionally provided useful information.

About once a month, Mrs. Murphy or Pewter would dispatch a field mouse or mole and dutifully drop it at Harry's feet, after which the attractive woman praised them lavishly. She never knew the difference, bragging to her friends about how she never saw a mouse in her house or barn. Well, she never did.

Having finally pried out the oddly shaped light bulb, Harry turned it around in her hand. "How am I supposed to find something like this?"

"*Go to Eck,*" Tucker said, sensibly suggesting an electrical supply firm because Harry would never find such a replacement bulb at Wal-Mart.

Harry glanced down as the dog offered unintelligible advice, then looked up again.

"*Car!*" Tucker immediately charged out the tack room's animal door, then charged back in. "*Coop!*"

"*I could have told you that,*" Pewter said, sprawled on the desk behind the offending lamp.

"*It's my job to announce any intruder or visitor,*" Tucker said. "*I am good at my work.*" The corgi pouted for a moment.

"*You are,*" Mrs. Murphy complimented the dog, then looked behind the tack trunk and addressed Martha the mouse. "*I can't control what she says. Cover your children's ears.*"

Cooper entered the tack room and took a look around. "Is this another Haristeen project?"

Harry motioned for her to sit in one of the director's chairs. "You can call it that. I will never buy anything based on design again."

Cooper, studying the lamp on its side, said, "Pain in the ass. All this fabulous-looking stuff. Like Gucci high heels that torture the feet. Just a royal pain. I'm ready to break out the oil lamps."

"I have them for emergencies. The smell isn't all that bad but the little plume of smoke will have you scrubbing ceilings and walls."

"If it's dark, you won't see it," Cooper laughed. "Less light now anyway. Every day gets shorter until December twenty-first, the solstice."

Harry dropped her hands into her lamp. "Always gets me a little." Then she handed the light bulb to her neighbor. "Look at this."

Bringing the tiny bulb close to her eyes, Cooper said, "To get another one of these, you'll have to go into town, spend time and burn gas. Oil lamps, I'm telling you, and think what we'd save on electricity."

"My darned electric bill for the house, the barn, and the big shed ran me over five hundred dollars last month, and you know that figure will go up with the darkness. Electric bills never get cheaper."

"Nope," Cooper said. "Of course, our entire society is dependent on it, and I'm as dependent as the next guy. Sometimes I wonder what kind of corner we have painted ourselves into."

"Me, too." Harry took the bulb back, placing it in the long desk drawer.

Pewter would knock it on the floor if Harry didn't hide it. She had to remember where she put it, though. Sometimes when a lot was happening all at once, Harry would forget the little things.

"I brought my seed book, thinking I'd swing by on my way home," said Coop.

"Where's the book?"

"Out in the car," Cooper said, standing. "I figured I'd ask first if you had the time."

"You don't have to ask. Go get it."

Within a few minutes the lanky police officer returned with a large, fat seed catalogue.

"*If they go through that whole thing, we will never get supper,*" said Pewter, mildly alarmed.

"*Do you some good.*" Tucker mischievously grinned.

Pewter sat up. "*I'm laying for you, Bubble Butt.*"

The dog ignored her as Mrs. Murphy left the tack trunk to sit next to Tucker, just in case.

Harry flipped through the pages, the glossy photos tempting her to think she, too, could grow such specimens. "So, what are you looking for, flowers or vegetables?"

"Buddy Janss promised me some corn seed and Miranda is giving me rose cuttings. And she said I could dig up that one Italian lilac bush she has."

"If it's Italian, don't do it," Harry laughed. "This damned lamp is Italian."

Cooper laughed with her. "I'll bear that in mind. You know the best varieties of okra, lettuce, all kinds of tomatoes. I don't know too much."

Harry read copy. "Okay. My advice"—she picked up a pencil and began circling vegetables—"is to go with the hardiest. Also, the old varieties often taste better but they're harder to grow sometimes. So, here." Harry pointed to a green pea. "A little water, a little sun. Tough. And so is this squash."

As Harry flipped through pages, circling types of vegetables, Cooper talked. "Both of our recent murder victims' bodies are with the medical examiner, but we already know how they were killed: bullet through the heart. No struggle, and the killer faced

Josh and Hester. So it's likely the killer seemed unthreatening, or they knew who it was and didn't fear him—or her."

"Face-to-face. Damn, that's cold-blooded."

"It is. I'm telling you because you found them. The paper will report the gunshot wounds, but we're holding back details, like face-to-face. No true bruises on the forearms, no teeth knocked out. You'd be surprised how many people fight for their lives, but neither Josh nor Hester fought, so I hope it was quick. Finding those victims always affects me. I wonder, were they afraid or was the adrenaline too high for them to act defensively? I guess it varies from person to person. One confusing moment of recognition when the gun was pulled, then *bam*."

Harry shivered. "It's still an awful thought."

"Well, this is more awful: If Hester knew her murderer, so do we. I think of that a lot, how many killers do I pass each day and don't know it?"

Harry rested her chin in her hand. "Never thought about that, but then, I'm not a deputy."

Cooper sighed. "Well, didn't mean to sound so negative. Back to the seeds."

"I marked everything you need, because I know your soils," said Harry. "You and I are both right up on the base of the mountains. We have our own little weather system."

Cooper took the catalogue back. "Thanks."

"This isn't negative exactly, but I can't erase the sight of both those people's grisly ends, and I didn't know how much I liked Hester until, well, until she wasn't with us," admitted Harry. "What could she have ever done to provoke being killed? I didn't know that accountant, but Hester wouldn't hurt anyone. Oh, she might make you check your watch, but she was okay."

"Best roadside stand in the county, and she'd always try to give me something for free," said Coop. "I'd tell her I can't take anything when I'm on duty. I mean, really, she wasn't bribing me, but the rules are rigid and people these days are so quick to find fault. If anyone had seen me take a cantaloupe and not pay, I bet you Rick or the newspaper would have heard about it."

"I can see the headline now: 'Scandalous Melon Payoff.'" Harry laughed.

"I'm starting to wonder if these aren't some sort of thrill killings. Usually sex is involved in those cases, or some sort of dominance or power play. This doesn't exactly fit the pattern, but then again, maybe we, the public, are supposed to feel a thrill, a ripple of fear."

Harry thought a long time. "So the killer is really warped or really smart, or both."

14

"*Poppy, she's not listening to you,*" Elocution warned as she sat in the chancery window the next morning, observing Harry outside.

Cazenovia and Lucy Fur meowed in unison.

Rev. Herb Jones, wedged behind his desk, glanced up, opening his mouth to quiet the kitties, then he heard a metallic clink. Pushing the chair away from his desk, he rose, hurrying to the window where Elocution fussed.

"*See! See!*" the cat spoke louder.

"I will bless her." Reverend Jones hustled out of his beautiful office, grabbing his coat and dashing out the back door. "Harry, what are you doing?" he said, finding her next to a ladder propped against the building's wall.

"Waiting for the roofer?" she half-fibbed.

"You were going to climb up there, I know it." Reverend Jones's face reddened.

"Well, eventually." She flashed her brightest smile.

Inside, Lucy Fur turned to Elocution. "*He can never resist her smile.*" Cazenovia agreed. "*It's amazing.*"

Outside, Harry, hands in pockets for the air had chilled, headed off a lecture. "Seth Isman will be here in a minute. I just know bad weather is around the corner, so I figured we'd better hop on this."

"Uh-huh." The reverend crossed his arms over his chest. "Hop on, hop up."

"Don't worry about me. I've got two feet on the ground and am looking at the most wonderful Lutheran minister in Virginia."

He burst out laughing. "You stinker." Then he put his arm around her. "Sweetie, I do thank you for taking on building and grounds and for doing this so soon after finding Hester's body. We would all have understood if you'd waited." He took a deep breath. "God rest her soul."

"I'd already made the appointment for today, Reverend, and truthfully, I feel better if I'm busy."

"You know, Hester's service still isn't organized." The pastor shook his head. "Hester's brother died years ago and her niece lives in Houston. I called over to St. Francis in Staunton, where Hester worshipped, but so far, no plans. We are all distressed. If I knew her niece I'd offer help, but Hester's priest told me the young lady—her name is Sarah Price—is doing all she can and he feels things will be properly done. She'll get here from Texas next week. Terrible. Such a terrible thing." He turned as the roofing van drove up and parked in the rear of the church lot. "Now, see here, Harry, don't you get up on that roof. Look me in the face and promise."

Taking a deep breath, she promised, "I won't."

"You can't dissemble to my face." He laughed. "Well, you can't really lie anyway. Never could, but that doesn't prevent you from withholding information or wiggling just a little."

"You've known me too long."

"Remember that. I've got my eye on you."

True to her word, Harry remained earthbound while wiry Seth

scrambled around up on the roof. After a few minutes, he backed down the ladder.

"Is it worse than I thought?" asked Harry of the short young man.

"No," he replied. "A two-foot-square area, just like you thought, should fix the problem and prevent more. The workmanship on that old roof is something, just something."

"Our ancestors knew what they were doing and they weren't deluded by technology. It still takes good materials and a good man who knows how to use them."

Seth smiled, which enlivened his strong face. "Yeah. We're losing it, though. Losing hand skills."

"You haven't lost yours," Harry complimented him.

"Thanks, Harry. Once I decided to concentrate on older structures, things just fell into place. I don't work with cheap materials. After I've repaired a roof, I don't get calls back about leaking. I understand that most folks don't know about construction. And they only have so much money, so they buy footage and flash instead of maybe something smaller that is well built. Being able to get up on this roof, seeing how those shingles were laid . . . I don't know. Kinda gives me chills. Like I'm part of something that goes way back."

"I know what you mean. Well, you know I have to report to the board, so as soon as you can write up an estimate, I will deliver it. They already agreed for the work to be done, but if I can present an estimate, that makes everyone feel better."

"You'll save money because I can do this with just one other man. We can work pretty fast together. The really good news is I have a source of slate shingles that should closely match yours. A huge old house was dismantled in Cumberland County. The heirs just let it go. Built in 1719." He paused. "A little bit of history slips away but it takes money to restore and keep those old places going.

I understand, but if you can't do it, sell it to someone who can. Don't wait until it falls apart."

"Good advice, but when there's more than one heir, things tend to get dragged out."

"Boy, that's the truth. Anyway, I can get on this next Monday. Figure a full day just in case. If all goes well, half a day. I don't think the bill will go over four thousand dollars, and I will try to do it for less. Preacher's price." He smiled broadly.

"Seth, you're a good egg."

"You don't know me," he devilishly replied. "Want me to put the ladder back?"

"Sure. Thank you. I'll walk with you to the shed."

As Harry and Seth strolled away, chatting about SEC football, she noticed Neil Jordan drive up, followed soon after by Wesley Speer.

After Seth drove away, Harry returned to the chancery.

"*There's a lift to her step,*" Lucy Fur noted. "*Must be good news.*"

"*We'll see.*" Cazenovia hopped off the windowsill to hurry out of the room and down the hall to greet Harry, whom she very much liked.

Pushing open the back door, Harry beheld the beautiful long-haired calico cat already on her hind legs.

"Caz." Harry knelt down and scooped her up. "Such a religious kitty. And such a good concierge."

"*I am.*"

Carrying the contented cat, Harry peered into the large office. She didn't want to disturb the reverend, as he seemed to be in the middle of a meeting. Neil and Wesley sat in the chairs around the coffee table. The reverend was standing at his desk, papers in hand. He looked up at her.

"I can come back," said Harry.

"No, come on in."

Putting Cazenovia down, Harry pulled off her work gloves. "Hi." Neil and Wesley stood up to greet her.

"Should I brace for the worst?" Neil joked.

"No. Good news. Seth can start on the roof next Monday, should finish the same day, and—here's the good part—he's got a source of old slate shingles and he feels sure he can keep the bill under four thousand. What luck."

"I suppose if a bill can be said to be good, that is," Neil solemnly replied.

"Neil, slate costs an arm and a leg," said Wesley. "Old slate, especially. We'll make up the shortfall if we have one, but I bet we don't." He beamed.

"Harry, sit down. Let's all have a hot cup of cocoa or whatever. Betty!" Reverend Jones called.

A middle-aged woman stuck her head in the room. "Yes? Oh, hi, everyone."

"How about cocoa?" The reverend looked at his small gathering.

"Cocoa sounds perfect." Harry smiled.

"I'll go with that," Wesley agreed, as did Neil.

The young, pretty secretary usually outside the reverend's office was now in her last months of pregnancy and on leave. Filling in was Betty Maddox, cousin to Dorothy, the sheriff's department's chief of forensics. You had to be careful what you said about people in Crozet, as most folks were related.

"While we wait, it's good you're here, Harry," said Neil. "I'd like to give the church lawns a good dressing of fertilizer and put it down before mid-November. Give it plenty of time to get into the ground. Checked the soil. Good pH, selenium. Potassium okay. Needs a little magnesium."

"Neil, that's wonderful." Harry smiled. "The little minidrought that we had didn't affect our lawns too much, but fertilizer always helps, and I'll come on back in springtime and drill in some wonderful lush grass seed. I always throw some rye in, too. Give the clover and bluegrass early cover."

Thanks to his real estate company, Wesley kept up with farming news. His largest sales were big estates and he had to know something about soil conditions and crop yields if selling to a true farmer, or even a new person who would lease out the land. Most new people wanted to live on a grand estate but didn't want to actually farm, which was wise since they weren't raised to it.

"Harry, did you see where the USDA"—he used the initials for the United States Department of Agriculture—"predicts the drought reduced our economic growth by almost half a percentage point? That's extremely serious."

"Sure is," she agreed. "But I was talking to Buddy Janss and he said what was so bizarre was that sometimes fields on one side of a road twisted up while on the other side the crops were healthy. What crazy weather. Buddy has suffered some losses, though."

Neil didn't much like Buddy, in part because the large fellow didn't buy his fertilizer. Buddy was so smart he'd worked out a deal years ago with horse owners to remove their manure and straw for free. This he put in piles, let it cook, then the next year used it himself, selling the extra for fertilizer. The horse owners, most of them owning but a few horses, gladly paid him to haul off the muck. Buddy used commercial fertilizers if a field needed extra potassium or another nutrient. That drove Neil crazy, but then, the two possessed such differing personalities they would have struggled to like each other no matter what. Neil was detail oriented and picky, whereas Buddy was expansive, and did his best but didn't fret.

"Wasn't Buddy friends with Hester?" Neil asked, as he had only lived in the area a few years.

"For years and years." Harry smiled. "You know Hester

wouldn't sell anything that was sprayed or if the seeds had been genetically modified."

"She was a crank," Neil said. "Not that I wished her dead, but really."

"Hester was an eccentric," the reverend said in his most diplomatic tone, "but she worked hard for causes she believed in, she mentored younger people like Tazio, and I expect any of us could be considered a crank at one time or another."

"Not you." Harry grinned and the men laughed.

"*You should live with him,*" Elocution called out from her fuzzy den on the floor.

"*He feeds us Fancy Feast and he even tried to see if we'd chew on greenies,*" Cazenovia chided her from the windowsill. "*He's the best.*"

"*Yeah, Elo,*" Lucy Fur chimed in. "*Button your lip.*"

"*All right, all right,*" the Lutheran cat said, giving in.

Betty arrived with a tray of hot cocoa and sugar cookies. The Reverend Jones jumped up to carry it and place it on the table.

Wesley returned to the subject of Hester. "Horrible. Harry, you have endured two shocks. Finding that young man and then Hester."

"Did," she agreed. "As I didn't know the fellow who was killed, it was a shock and that was all, but Hester, that hurt. Yes, she had her ways, but she was a good soul and really pretty smart. I mean a lot smart, actually."

"That she was," Wesley agreed. "The last time I stopped by the stand, we got on the subject of crop irrigation. I don't remember how we did get on it—you know with Hester, one thing didn't lead to another, it jumped to another. But anyway, she was telling me that farmers have been pulling water out of the Ogallala Aquifer since the early 1950s and some of those irrigation booms are a half mile long. A half mile!"

"Great day," Reverend Jones exclaimed.

"It's hard to imagine, isn't it?" said Wesley. "A half-mile boom spinning around a fixed water pipe? But there's a lot of talk, consideration in a lot of the affected states, about cutting back on irrigation because the droughts are dropping water levels, as is all the population growth."

"Where are water levels dropping? Which states?" Neil asked.

Fortified by the cocoa, Wesley leapt in. "Neil, it's eastern Wyoming, about all of Nebraska, southern South Dakota, eastern Colorado and New Mexico, a huge swath of Kansas, Oklahoma's Panhandle, and a chunk of Texas. The water shortage is huge."

"The breadbasket," Harry thought out loud.

"For us. For the world, too, really," Wesley said. "Hester had been reading up on it, just like she was always reading about chemicals, her history interests, that sort of thing. I was so impressed at the facts she had at her fingertips. She felt if farmers didn't cut back, wells would run dry and that would become a disaster, a true disaster. Irrigation accounts for one-third of our nation's annual water demand. I told her that genetic engineering could create more drought-tolerant corn, soybeans, etc. We could reduce our irrigation, but she didn't want to hear that."

They laughed.

Harry stood up. "It was good to see you all and I'm glad I have what I think is good news about the roof. Tell you what we could do for Hester: Let's sell all those tickets for the Halloween Hayride. The funds go to the library, and we know how much Hester loved the Crozet Library. Will you all help me?"

"It would be an honor," Wesley immediately replied.

"Of course," Neil agreed.

In his gravelly voice, the Reverend Jones said, "I can preach a good sermon on this. We'll sell those tickets. We'll sell out! Thou hast put gladness in my heart." He smiled. "Psalm 4:7. If we sell those tickets, it will put gladness in all our hearts."

15

"How many miles have you racked up on this car?" Harry asked later that day. The two friends were headed back to that shopping mecca, Warehouse Number 9.

In the driver's seat, Susan glanced down at her Audi's odometer. "Let's see . . . 131,839. I'm averaging about 40,000 miles per year. Engines are so well made these days they aren't even broken in until 100,000 miles."

Swaying slightly as they turned right at the stoplight in Dillwyn on Route 20, Harry said, "True. The advances in engine longevity are pretty fabulous. 'Course, my old '78 rolls along, but I baby that truck, as you know. Actually, Susan, I really like driving without computer chips."

"That's you. I don't care." Susan smiled. "Is everyone asleep back there? It's so quiet without the cats."

Harry twisted to look. "Owen is curled up with his sister Tucker. That was one of the best litters you ever bred."

"It was." Susan nodded. "I loved breeding corgis, but it was so much work, and part of that work was making sure the puppies found the right homes. I love all dogs but I especially love corgis."

"I love Tucker. Sometimes I think about the German shepherd

Mom and Dad had when I was a kid. That was a great dog. Funny how you can measure your life by animal lives."

"Wonder if that scarecrow fellow had any pets."

"No. Coop told me he lived an unencumbered life."

"Sad," Susan replied simply.

"I think so, too. What's the purpose of being alive if you don't have husbands, friends, cats, dogs, horses, birds, possums, more friends, and friends' children? It just goes on and on. Mother used to say that if everyone in Virginia studied their bloodlines, we'd find out we are related. No one is all black, no one is all white. We're all part of one another and that includes the Indians."

"Can't say 'Indian' anymore."

"Sure about that? These labels we give ourselves are always changing."

"Now, Harry. You look just like your father when you get muley."

"Do I?"

"Exactly."

"Oh, dear." Harry slumped in her seat slightly. "Daddy could be . . ."

"Yes, he could."

They both laughed, remembering Harry's much-loved and very original father.

"Today is going to be a mob scene at the store. People are feeling that change in the seasons, the holidays looming. Those credit cards start burning in one's pocket."

"Not mine," Harry staunchly declared.

"It is possible to be too tight. I mean, Harry, you don't have voice messaging on your phone because it costs an extra three dollars a month. That's silly. Three dollars!"

"A penny saved is a penny earned," Harry countered.

"'Tis, but you can carry it too far. Hey, where do I turn?"

"Left up ahead."

Susan turned onto the Farmville main drag, then turned left again at Harry's direction, and shortly the Audi station wagon was parked in the lot closest to Number 9 warehouse. As predicted, the place was packed.

Susan cracked the windows for the two dogs, although the day was brisk. "You all go back to sleep. We won't be long." She hoped this wasn't a fib. She loved looking at furniture, fabrics, even lampshades.

The two women walked into Number 9, and Harry immediately pulled Susan to the Halloween display.

"Exactly the same," Harry declared.

"As I didn't see the corpse in the cornfield, I can only imagine what a human looked like as opposed to this."

"But that's just it. From a distance, they look exactly the same."

Susan stood next to the ghosts. "No witches."

"Not in this display. It's ghosts, little goblins, pumpkins, and the scarecrow." Harry sat down in a kitchen chair for a moment. "You know, I think of Hester hanging all that black and orange bunting at the stand, then last week trussing herself up in a witch costume while unloading produce. She did have such a funny sense of things, and you had to laugh. Why would anyone kill her? I've thought of everything, including her being a Russian spy. I mean wild stuff. Nah." Harry shook her head.

"Me, too." Susan looked around. "I'm going to walk through the floor. Won't be long."

"I'll tag along." Harry did.

"Look at this." Susan pointed out a distressed bureau painted a sky blue. "That would look good in my workroom."

"What do you need with a bureau in your workroom?"

"Store papers in it. Better looking than a file cabinet."

"Yeah, I guess. Here." Harry handed her a notebook and pencil from her coat pocket. "Write down the particulars. If you decide you want it, you can call. They deliver."

"I forgot about that." Susan scribbled down the item number and manufacturer.

Harry again tacked over to the Halloween display. "Whoever killed Josh Hill had to have seen this scarecrow. It looks exactly the same. So the killer is someone who comes through here regularly."

"Maybe. It could also be someone with a good memory or someone who took a picture on their phone. That could be just about anyone."

"You're right. I'm jumping to conclusions."

"They should make that an Olympic sport." Susan put her hand under Harry's elbow to steer her out of the store.

They walked over to Number 8, which had a courtyard featuring large outdoor sculptures for sale.

"I like the large horse." Harry stood next to an almost life-sized horse resembling the horses of Piazza San Marco. "Can you imagine what would happen if I put one by the barn?"

Both women laughed. They knew the statue would spook the real horses, although eventually they would adjust.

Susan flipped the price tag over. "You'll need smelling salts."

Harry bent over to peer at the tag. "Nine thousand dollars!"

"You pay for your pleasures." Susan checked her watch. "Speaking of which, if I stay here, I am going to spend money, and I don't have it right now. Ned isn't making as much at the law firm. He's in session and there goes the income. He thought he could swing it, but there's so much to do down in Richmond, so many meetings and so much material to master, plus he had to rent an apartment. It's overwhelming. Yet he loves being in our House of Delegates. Anyway, I'm thinking of finding a job."

Once they were back in the car and heading home, Harry said, "Your kids are out of the house. No reason you can't work full-time."

"When we graduated from college and I got my first job as a legal assistant, I remember shopping in the supermarket, seeing the women at the checkout counters and wondering what went wrong. You know what I mean? How did they wind up in that job?"

"I never thought about it. You were, *are*, better about that stuff than I am." Harry put on her sunglasses.

"Well, I thought maybe those cashiers had picked the wrong man. He'd left them high and dry and with children. Or they were people who didn't plan ahead and one day woke up at forty. As years rolled along, I realized that sometimes bad luck rolls over someone like a tide. I felt less superior after that. Now I look at those women and think it could be me, you know?"

Harry thought for a long time. "I don't. Susan, I always knew I would farm."

"But what if the crop failed year after year? What if you became injured?"

"I have had crops fail and I survived, on not much. I figure whatever happens, I can deal with it. 'Course, it's easier now with Fair. My hardest times were without him."

"It preys on my mind, finding Hester like that," said Susan. "She never expressed fears. But I think maybe her ideas—like aliens being responsible for crop circles, stuff like that—maybe that was how she expressed fear."

"Susan, you might be right. I don't know. I don't look into other people like you do or like Fair does; I kind of take everyone at face value."

"*What if they're hiding behind a mask?*" Tucker wondered.

16

Although two hundred and twenty years old, the organ at St. Luke's sounded as good as the day it was installed, twenty years after the church's cornerstone was laid, and possibly even better, for time had enriched the sounds. The early small congregations had worked tirelessly to afford such a wonderful organ. Subsequent generations of worshippers continued to give thanks.

This Sunday morning, even Cazenovia, Lucy Fur, and Elocution luxuriated in the deep reverberations of the low notes, the sparkle of the high. While Reverend Jones delivered his sermon, the three cats sat in the balcony along with the organist and the robed choir. Occasionally the choir would sing down below, but somehow their voices always sounded better from the balcony. As the cats often attended services, none of the choir members paid them any mind.

Lucy Fur listened as her human's deep voice filled the church. *"Poppy worked so hard on this sermon."*

"He likes any story about people helping people," said Elocution. *"I don't think there are Bible stories about people helping animals."*

Cazenovia added her two cents: *"There's lots of stories about us helping them. All the animals in the stable, and how about the donkey that carried Jesus on his last journey?"*

"*We helped build Christianity,*" said Lucy Fur. "*I mean, how about all the disciples? They had to travel. Donkeys and mules carried them or carted them, too. Dogs protected them and cats kept the grain supply free from pests. All the saints would have died young if it weren't for us.*"

"*That's too long ago and far away,*" said Elocution. "*How about all we did to create the United States? We saved the colonists time and again, and then when we went to war against Great Britain, animals fought and suffered, too. Cats are perfect spies. The problem was the humans didn't listen. We could have shortened the war.*"

Cazenovia smiled. "*Poppy reads aloud, and remember when he read about those battles lost in South Carolina? But it all turned out all right. We're here.*"

As the Reverend Jones preached about humans seeing beyond one another's superficial differences and helping others, the cats convinced themselves of their own superiority.

Once the service ended, Reverend Jones walked down the center aisle to the door at the back of the church. As the congregants exited, he shook the hand of each one, chatting with them a few moments.

Harry had always liked this part of the service.

As this was the eleven o'clock service, the crowd of worshippers poured out onto the grounds a bit after twelve noon. The temperature had risen to sixty-two degrees; it was a gorgeous October day, the leaves in flaming color.

BoomBoom and her partner, Alicia, chatted with Susan and Ned. Groups formed and re-formed as different folks caught up with one another.

Neil Jordan moved from group to group, selling tickets to the Halloween Hayride. Whether they intended to go or not, everybody bought one.

"Harry, Fair," he greeted them. "Tickets?"

"We bought five," said Harry. "I bought them from Hester." She

thought about that for a moment, then recovered. "But tell you what. If you give me a handful, I'll sell them this week."

"Harry, I only have twenty left." He beamed.

"Ah. I'll get more from the library, then. That's wonderful, Neil."

"Eighty tickets." He couldn't resist telling the number he'd sold. "I'll have these twenty sold in no time."

"You're a big success." Fair slapped him on the back.

Before he left them, Neil said, "Harry, I want to bring you materials on some different kinds of fertilizer I have. If you fertilize now in the fall, it's perfect. And if you've planted winter wheat or cold-resistant rye, you will be amazed at the yield. I know you're busy, but I'm really high on these new types of fertilizer applications. The normal corn yield in a good year is about 207 bushels per acre without irrigation. My fields yielded 250 and my irrigated fields averaged 320 per acre. And this wasn't a particularly good year. If you like my products, we can work out a payment plan."

"Sure. I'll call you."

He persisted. "I rented two thousand acres in Nelson County to show what these fertilizers can do. I numbered the strips just like you do with corn varieties. You just wait. Next year's numbers will soar." With that and a big smile, Neil left.

Walking with her husband toward BoomBoom and Alicia, Harry remarked, "He'll soon have as many acres under cultivation at Buddy Janss."

Fair shrugged. "Neil seems to thrive on competition, on a task, I guess."

"Hey, wasn't that a great sermon?" Alicia, a former movie star now in her fifties, hugged Fair.

The old friends all started talking at once as soon as Susan and Ned joined them.

"My wife told me you'll start on the roof tomorrow," Ned said to Harry.

"Be done before nightfall."

"Susan said that Seth has old slate shingles," said the Richmond politician, with respect.

"Ned, I think he has everything. He doesn't even bother with the salvage yards. He has lines to those small companies dismantling old buildings or rebuilding historic ones that can be saved."

"Smart. I think there's a real niche for that kind of business. It's not all big companies. I keep trying to push in the House for the small businessman, the artisans, and little by little some of my colleagues are getting it."

Fair smiled. "You can't always shoot the stag, but you can still eat if you bring home a lot of rabbits."

The group smiled and nodded.

BoomBoom then said, "Sometimes I think small is better. I go to the bank now, the same bank I have used for twenty-five years, it's been bought up and amalgamated so many times that even though the tellers all know me, I have to go through hoops! I can't even transfer money from my personal account to my business account without paperwork. My money!"

Alicia put her hand on BoomBoom's forearm, since she knew a tirade was dangerously close. "If it's too big to fail, it's too big to exist," she said.

That got them all going.

On the way home in Fair's vet truck, Harry fluffed her plaid wrap skirt. "Don't you love our friends? We can talk about anything and I always learn something. And I love that we can agree to disagree."

"Me, too."

"Yesterday at a meeting in the chancery, Neil described Hester as a wacko. Well, maybe he didn't put it that strongly, but we let him know in the nicest way that, yes, she was a little strange, but she was part of Crozet and she did much good. Now he's hawking those tickets. Maybe this is atonement."

"Well, that would be nice," said Fair. "My experience of Neil is he assumes we're all dumb rednecks."

"If he wants his fertilizer business to thrive, he'd better get used to it. And you don't go into fertilizer if you want to discuss Raphael," said Harry, an art history major at Smith.

Fair laughed. "You have a lot to answer for."

"Oh," she mused, "Mother thought whatever I did was fine, but Dad sure was surprised. He'd say, 'How can you make a dime being an art history major?' And I'd say, 'Dad, this is the only time in my life when I can study, when I don't have to make money. I'll come back to the farm.'" She paused. "Little did I know they'd both be gone by the beginning of my junior year."

"You never know. I loved your parents. We all did."

They drove along in silence, then Harry thought out loud, "Do you think anyone ever loved Hester like that?"

A long silence followed. "No," he answered at last. "But she was part of all of us, she was valued. That counts for something."

Turning down the long gravel driveway, Harry added, "Alicia was telling me to read a book about the environment. And then she told me to pick up one that's a few years old, *The Great Warming*."

"She's always been a big reader," said Fair.

"She said that back in her acting days, there was so much downtime on the sets that she made up for not going to college with one book after another." Harry saw a redheaded woodpecker dart along the fence line. "I hope our fences don't have bugs."

"I doubt it. That pesky fellow is heading for the next tree. You know, sometimes I look at Alicia and I think what a terrific vet she would have made, or a professor. She does read all the time and she wants to learn. A real passion for knowledge."

"She always told me she hated Hollywood. She felt like a piece of meat. The money was great, but through her, I learned about the sorrows of great beauty."

He turned to look at her. "You don't have any?"

At this she let out a war whoop.

Sunday afternoon, Harry and Fair, accompanied by Mrs. Murphy, Pewter, and Tucker, tackled laying out all the heavy-duty extension cords, hooking them up at various places, and running them out to large water troughs in the smaller fenced pastures. The water troughs had heaters in them, and though conditions were mild, it was best to do this before heavy frosts arrived.

The largest pasture, seventy good acres, lay along the creek between Harry's farm and Coop's, so it didn't need a trough.

The horses happily drank from the clear flowing mountain waters, for Harry had extended some fencing onto Coop's side so they could easily wade around, which they enjoyed. Coop thought that was just fine. Most country people worked at accommodation. The trouble began when an outsider bought an old farm and for whatever reason felt no need to share. They seemed to think that people wanted to take advantage of them and that boundary lines were sacrosanct. Naturally, this created problems and often the newcomers found they had few friends except for other newcomers. Then something awful would happen and their neighbors would show up to help out. It usually changed their attitude. They figured out why their neighbors, whom they had usually disturbed or offended in some fashion, showed up to help. It was the country way. Most learned to be a little country themselves. A few did not and returned to where they had originated or moved on, looking for the next wondrous place. Perhaps this happened all over the country, but it happened in Virginia a lot, probably due to the state's great beauty. People wanted to live there.

Harry thought all this as she checked her lines. If Coop couldn't eventually buy the old Jones place and if Reverend Jones one day had to sell, she could be facing this problem.

There were problems enough for now.

She and Fair finished the day's work, ate supper, then took a sunset walk all the way back to the vast walnut groves Susan owned on this side of the Blue Ridge Mountains.

A barred owl flew from one tree to another.

"So silent," Harry noted.

"And such an efficient hunter," Fair added.

"I'm just *as good*," Pewter bragged from below, never one to tolerate compliments of others.

From a perch high above, the owl looked down at this groundling. "*Dream on.*"

"*I'll show you,*" Pewter sassed, "*and furthermore, you don't come around the barn because Flatface is bigger than you.*"

Flatface, the great horned owl, lived in the cupola. She was two and a half feet high. The barred owl was about a foot and a half, with a wingspan just under four feet, impressive enough on his own terms.

"*Pewter, I wouldn't start a fight with an owl, even a screech owl,*" Tucker wisely admonished.

"*Hoo!*" the barred owl replied.

And down below, Harry, once again thinking of who could have killed Hester, thought, "Who, indeed?"

17

"*W*hy are we going this way?" Pewter asked as she stared out the station wagon window Monday evening. "I'm ready to go home."

"*We've only been on the road for fifteen minutes*," Mrs. Murphy replied. "*Plus you just ate fresh tuna. Don't be crabby.*"

"*I'm not crabby!*" Pewter snapped. "*I just want to know what she's doing, that's all. She checked the roof work at St. Luke's and now she's heading west—the wrong direction. You know how she can get if she sees a friend or passes one on the road.*" The gray cat referred to Harry's conviviality; her human was always stopping to chew the fat with another local.

Also staring out the window, Tucker said, "*She had to get to St. Luke's before sunset. She wanted to recheck the roof work.*"

"*The roof work is fine,*" Pewter spoke louder.

The three watched as Harry slowed, then turned in to the old gravel driveway to the three abandoned school buildings.

"*Hey, there's Brinkley.*" Tucker stood on her hind legs as she saw her yellow Lab friend sitting in front of the faded clapboard building with paint peeling.

After parking, Harry stepped out, then opened the door for the animals, all of whom rushed to the big sweet dog.

"Hey," Tazio Chappars called out as Harry stepped through the schoolhouse door, which creaked.

Harry looked around. "I've never been in here."

"Few people have after 1965, I guess." Tazio dropped her hand to pet Brinkley's head. "What do you think?"

"Has character. Public buildings don't anymore. Plus they look so cheap. Ugly boxes."

"You're talking to an architect." Tazio laughed. "'Ugly' is too kind a word. And these three distinguished buildings were built for the underclass, for lack of a better word. We have beautiful examples throughout the state of what was built for the middle classes and the rich. Maybe builders had a better feel back then for space, light, warm materials. I don't find reinforced concrete warm." She smiled. "Hester railroaded me. Now I'm going to railroad you, girl."

"Let me sit down." Harry sat at one of the old-fashioned desks and took a deep breath. "I'm ready. Have at me."

Tazio sat at the desk across from Harry, as she once had done with Hester. "You know so many people. Your people have been here since the Revolutionary War. They've worshipped at St. Luke's since that time."

Harry crossed her arms over her chest. "With a lead-in like that, this is going to be a biggie. I know it."

"Uh, yes." Tazio leaned toward Harry a bit. "I believe Hester knew she was going to die." Tazio held up her hand, sensing that Harry was about to interrupt her. "She knew she was in danger. When she asked me to take on the fight—the project of bringing these buildings back to life—I said I would only do it if she led the charge. She agreed but then she made me promise before we parted that if something happened to her, I would carry on."

"Dear God." Harry's hand flew to her face.

"It's a promise I must fulfill. I, well, I just must."

"Of course, Tazio. It's a debt of honor, and think of how much she trusted you."

"I do."

"You told this to Cooper?"

"I did. Gives her not one more solid fact, but she did say it's possible Hester knew more than she was telling. We'll never know, but what I want to know is, will you work with me, Harry, use your contacts to help save the schoolhouses?"

Harry thought a bit, then replied, "I will, but you and I have to be clear about the future use of the buildings. That means involving other people, asking their opinions, and, well, I don't want to put the cart before the horse. Let's do the Halloween Hayride first. I see you've started on Frankenstein's table."

Harry looked at the red lights that accentuated the fake pools of plastic cut-out blood on the table and floor. Strangely cut lampshades cast ominous shadows with low light.

A flat table, straps across it, stood in the middle of the classroom. Tazio had moved some of the desks aside to make room for it. "This is the mad doctor's operating room," she stated with faux solemnity.

"Sure looks convincing," said Harry.

"Good. I want to make this year special," said Tazio. "This has to be the best Halloween Hayride ever. Raise tons of money for the library."

"Who is going to be Frankenstein, or will he be a cutout figure?" Harry inquired.

"Buddy Janss volunteered to be the monster. Wesley Speer said he'd be the doctor. Has a lab coat, sort of, and clothes they wore back in Mary Shelley's time."

"Wesley Speer. Good for him." Harry smiled at the thought of her fellow vestry board member being Dr. Frankenstein.

"I heard that Neil Jordan has sold one hundred hayride tickets in just a few days," said Tazio. "That's something. He must be twisting every arm he knows."

"He can be persuasive, and it is a tradition. Also, in a sick way, the scarecrow and the witch deaths have kind of promoted the horror aspect, driving up sales." Harry looked around. "Built solid, this schoolhouse."

"All three of them have stood the test of time. One for the little children, then the middle school, and the last building was for the big kids. I went through drawers and found old test tubes and stuff. I'm going to set it all up, see if I can't get some things smoking and bubbling and then backlight it."

"Creepy and perfect. However, don't let Brinkley in. That tail could be lethal."

"I'll put everything over his head. I learned the hard way, he can clean off a coffee table. He'd make a real mess in here."

As though on cue, Brinkley pushed open the front door, letting in a rush of cold air. *"I'm here. I'm watching everything."*

"What can you see?" Pewter said, marching in behind. *"My eyes are a lot better than yours."*

Brinkley, a natural diplomat, replied, *"They are. I wish I could see as good in the dark as you and Mrs. Murphy do."*

Harry walked to the door to close it. "Boy, that temperature drops with the sun."

"That's another thing," said Tazio. "This old heating system works. I checked it out, cast iron. The boiler is enormous but solid cast iron. The boiler room was installed right about the time of World War One."

Harry wondered, "Who would know how to repair the boiler?"

"Same company's been servicing it since installing it in 1915. Couldn't stand it—I hopped on my computer, and sure enough, the information is online."

"That's a piece of luck." Harry smiled.

Tazio agreed. "It is. Harry, thank you for signing on. You and I will make a great team. I hope Hester's looking down on us and giving a cheer."

"Me, too, but she might be saying, 'Not Harry!'"

Tazio smiled. "Not a chance. Well, I think we've got the ride in good order."

"This ride scares me before I even get on the hay wagon." Harry's eyes widened. "It's going to be spectacular."

"Let me show you the little bathroom." Tazio stood up.

The two walked to the door at the back of the large room. Tazio opened it.

"Water still runs." Harry turned the faucet on and off. "The old towel dispenser still works, too." She gave the white towel a tug and more came down as the used portion fed up into the metal dispensing box. "Gets me excited. The quality of the workmanship, the layout."

They closed the door and walked to the front of the room. Harry, always curious, sat behind the large teacher's desk, which was set on a dais so the teacher could view the entire classroom.

"You will now recite your ABC's," Harry ordered.

Tazio, before her, ran through them quickly, then shoved Harry from the seat.

"Harry Haristeen, what is twelve times twelve?"

"One hundred and forty-four," Harry victoriously answered.

"I gave you an easy one," Tazio teased as she pulled out the middle desk drawer. "Hey, look."

Harry stepped back up on the dais. "Pencils, a hand sharpener, a wooden ruler."

"Grandpa's Tar Soap," Tazio said, reading the advertising printed on the ruler. "And here's an old piece of paper."

Harry read out the name printed on the paper: "Walter Ashby Plecker."

"If Walter's name was in the teacher's drawer, he must have been a bad boy," said Tazio.

18

*T*hursday, October 24, the service for Hester Martin was finally held at St. Francis Catholic Church in Staunton. Harry quietly sat in the pew, next to Susan, BoomBoom, Alicia, Big Mim, and Miranda Hogendobber. Fair, up in Leesburg at a veterinary conference, couldn't attend, but most everyone else who knew Hester was there. Wearing a suit, Buddy Janss made people look twice, since the portly farmer was nearly always seen wearing overalls.

Harry appreciated the dignity of the Catholic service. She thought that being a Lutheran, as she was, was sort of like being a Catholic but without the incense. In her mind, people divided up into high church and low church. She admired Miranda, staunch member of the Church of the Holy Light, a charismatic church, for her strong feeling of a personal relationship with God. But Harry needed the liturgy, the ritual. Obviously, Hester had needed it, too.

Fortunately, Hester's niece, Sarah Price, raised Catholic, had made sure the ceremony was done just right. She had spoken at length with the priest and had picked out appropriate hymns. A woman in her mid-thirties, Sarah quite resembled her eccentric aunt.

Hester's niece had relied on Susan Tucker to help her with the other necessary arrangements after finding her name in Hester's address book. She'd placed a gold star next to Susan's name. Hester used different colored stars and gold meant the best.

Sarah also had the presence of mind to give the address book to the sheriff.

As the mourners filed out after the service, they walked down steep steps to the parking lot below. Wesley Speer and Buddy assisted the elderly down the hazardous steps, the older folks grasping the railing for all they were worth.

Slowly descending next to Harry, Big Mim said, "Staunton is a town of hills. One can find a wonderful view for a reasonable price."

"True," Harry replied.

"Mary Baldwin has the best spot in town," remarked Boom-Boom, just behind them.

Mary Baldwin College did indeed have a wonderful setting. The prestigious school had been continually graduating women since 1842, and most of those alumnae had flourished, often bucking the odds against women.

Woodrow Wilson's house rested not far from the college, and Harry wondered whether as a boy he had watched the girls walk by. It was hard to imagine the former president as a man being dazzled by women. In photographs, he appeared rather cold.

"Well, on to the cemetery. It's really beautiful," Alicia noted. On the west side of town, the graveyard was a refuge for the living to think and reflect, and a fitting place for the departed.

The graveyard was glowing with October sunlight when Hester's Crozet friends reached it. Again, the burial service for the dead was dignified and brief.

The reception that followed was held in Hester's home and started at four. It took most of the crowd about forty-five minutes to drive to the simple brick two-story house, a graceful structure that had belonged to Hester's grandparents. The paint on the brick, a creamy yellow, had flaked in spots, and the soft paprika of old brick shone through. The old place felt warm and lived in.

Having never been inside Hester's house, Harry was curious to see it, and paused in the entryway.

Cooper, right next to her, also paused a moment. "Some of this furniture has to go back to the Revolution."

"Heppelwhite," Big Mim, close by, crisply filled her in. "And the silver is Georgian, but not just any George. George II."

"I had no idea," Harry exclaimed.

"That was her way." Big Mim removed her hat. "Hester lived simply. She wanted it that way."

Always proper, Big Mim wore a hat in church, as did most of the older women. Harry and Susan also wore hats, mostly because their mothers had long ago drummed it into them. Neither woman much liked hats.

Big Mim knew Hester better than the others. "She inherited most of what one needs in life. Not an ounce of the snob in her; she would never have called attention to the quality of the furnishings, the fabrics, and, of course, the elegant silver. I will miss her." The older woman smiled sorrowfully, then began moving about, a pure political animal regardless of circumstance. Big Mim was of that generation that worked through men. Her husband, Jim, was mayor of Crozet.

"Well, old girl, ready for the shake and howdy?" Harry teased Cooper, who had not been born and bred in the region.

"I'm getting ready." Cooper followed Harry.

Susan stood next to Sarah, introducing her to the guests.

"Sarah, please meet my best and oldest friend in the world,

Harry Haristeen, and with her, one of our sheriff's department deputies, Cynthia Cooper."

Sarah shook their hands. "Thank you so much for helping to celebrate my aunt's life."

"The service became her: simple and elegant," Harry complimented her.

Cooper stepped up to the plate. "And the gravesite is so beautiful."

"Thank you. Please have some refreshments," said Sarah. "Buddy Janss made the punch. He said it was my aunt's favorite."

The two moved on, glancing at each other with raised eyebrows.

Harry pushed Cooper through the crowd. "You first."

"I am not drinking that stuff."

"A sip. Come on, girl. You can do it."

They arrived at an enormous silver scalloped punch bowl; the family initials in elegant script were intertwined on its front.

Between laughter and tears, Buddy ladled out a full silver cup.

"Buddy," warned Coop, not yet committed to this alcoholic endeavor.

"Come on, Coop. You're not on duty."

"If I drink this, I will pass out," Coop protested.

"First your legs will lock up. But I'll carry you home," he promised.

He was irresistible, so Coop took a too-big swig. Harry wisely sipped hers.

Coop gasped. "My throat is on fire."

Buddy laughed. "Well, go on and talk to people. That will cool you down. Neil, come on, your turn."

Neil Jordan accepted a silver cup, drank a bit. His eyes watered. Reverend Jones squeezed in next to him and laughed.

"Did Hester really drink this stuff?" Neil sputtered. "My God, what a tough broad."

"You're just now figuring that out?" Reverend Jones slapped him on the back.

Neil didn't spill a drop. He reached into his pockets, pulled out tickets to the Halloween Hayride, and began moving through the crowd—with difficulty, but he was selling those tickets.

"Reverend, did you have a clue that Hester had such impeccable taste in home furnishings?" Harry asked as he was now pushed next to her.

"Well, I'd been here once or twice. Knew her people, of course, as did you. All of them quiet living. Well, you knew her mother and father and her older brother."

"I was pretty little and they seemed so old. I don't remember her brother except that he was tall," Harry responded.

The party grew louder as the punch took effect. Faces red, people in the crowd talked over one another as they each recalled their favorite Hester stories. Some burst into tears, but that's the way of a Virginia celebration. Emotions rise right up to the surface.

"She was not lonely," said the reverend. "People thought she was, because in this part of the world you march in twos. Crozet is a Noah's ark." The preacher took a sip, peered over the silver rim. "And, Coop, you'll be walking side by side with someone before you know it."

"Oh, I don't know."

"A good-looking woman like you? Just you wait." He beamed at her, then returned to the subject of Hester. "She threw herself into good works. I believe she was a fulfilled person, a good person. Granted, sometimes the notions about black gum trees or the fact that food modification would make us all idiots took me aback, but we all have our pet peeves."

As the conversation continued, Wesley Speer moved toward Buddy. A funeral gathering is as good a place as any to patch up hard feelings.

Buddy held out a full cup. "Wesley."

"Buddy, I've been pushing you a little hard about those one hundred acres. I'm overanxious."

Buddy took a deep breath. "Wesley, in these times I think we are all overanxious. Let's just set it aside for now and we can talk maybe after Thanksgiving. I can't sell rich soil without replacing it, you see?"

"I do, Buddy, I really do."

The two men clinked cups and Buddy then nodded to the next person pressing at the punch bowl.

"I can hardly breathe," Cooper whispered.

"What?" Harry inclined her ear toward her.

A bit louder, Coop repeated herself.

"It's the punch," said Harry. "It'll stay with you for a while. Don't drink any more," she advised.

"I'm sorry I drank what I did. This can't be legal." Cooper ruefully smiled.

"Well, dear Deputy, if you run a roadside stand and you've lived here all your life and your people have lived here since way back, your friends know where to find the best country waters to see you off with."

Cooper laughed as she saw her boss, Rick Shaw, the sheriff, come into the room. "He knows about the hooch, of course."

"Always did." Harry laughed. "It's a wise law enforcement officer who knows when to turn a blind eye."

"Ain't that the truth? Let's see if we can work our way over to the library. Doesn't look like so many people there."

The two edged their way through the crowd toward the

mahogany-shelved library, chatting as they did so, which meant the short walk into the next room took a half hour.

Just before reaching the library, Harry bumped into Cindy Walters, whom she introduced to Cooper.

"This is so terrible." Cindy spoke above the crowd noise. "I no sooner reached home than I turned around to come back. She would have done the same for me."

"Yes," Harry simply agreed.

Cindy looked at Cooper. "I don't know if this will help you but Hester told me she was stepping on toes. Her refusal to sell sprayed crops, her opposition to development. She mentioned this in passing."

"Any names?" Cooper was accustomed to people providing information.

"No."

"Did she seemed frightened?"

"Officer, I don't really know. Hester hid a lot."

"Thank you, Miss Walters."

"Where's Heidi?" Harry asked.

"Upstairs. Couldn't live without her." The short, trim lady smiled.

Once inside the library, they looked at the books, many old, bound in Moroccan leather of deep colors.

Harry found a shelf dealing with agriculture. "She's got books dating back to World War One; she's got books released year by year from the U.S. Department of Agriculture."

Coop bent down to read spines on the lower shelves. "Some of these are in French. Hey, here's one on Percherons and it looks very, very old."

Harry knelt down. "Percherons are French draft horses. I had no idea. I mean, I knew that Hester had a college degree, but look at all these books."

"Here're two rows on Indian affairs." Cooper squinted to see better.

Harry joined her and looked closely at the titles. "She must have everything Virginia and the U.S. government ever released on the subject."

"She's got newer stuff, too," said Coop. "Custer and Little Big Horn. *Bury My Heart at Wounded Knee.*" The law officer read a few more titles out loud, then moved to the next shelf at her eye level. She stopped cold. "Harry."

"Yeah?" Harry was utterly absorbed in her examination of the old volumes.

"Come here."

Harry did as she was asked and beheld a photograph of Hester in an old silver frame. She had a fly rod in her hand, and her surroundings looked to be Bath or Highland County, Virginia counties adjacent to the state of West Virginia. Standing next to her in a stream was a man considerably younger, fishing rod also in hand. He held up a lovely trout.

Harry leaned closer.

"It's Josh Hill," Cooper said, her voice low.

Harry swallowed. "I never saw his face, I mean intact."

Cooper had seen plenty of photographs of the accountant during her ongoing research. "It's him all right, which makes me wonder: Were these two fishing for trouble together?"

19

$\mathcal{S}$unlight flooded Hester's kitchen, which faced east. The morning after the reception, Cooper and Rick Shaw sat at the kitchen's small square wooden table with Sarah Price. After apologizing for troubling her at such a time, the two law enforcement officers began their questioning of Hester Martin's niece.

"Did you ever meet the young man in the photograph?" Rick Shaw asked Sarah. The silver-framed photo of Hester and Josh Hill sat on the table in front of them.

"Not that I remember," the pleasant woman replied. "I don't know who he is."

"She never mentioned Josh Hill?" asked Rick.

Sarah looked again at the photo. "No."

"Did she talk about fishing?" Cooper asked.

"Some. Aunt Hester and I would speak over the phone about once a week. She wouldn't text me or email. She said she wanted to hear my voice, then she'd know if I was okay."

"Did she talk about her other interests?" Rick folded his hands then unfolded them.

"Aunt Hester loved to lecture! That is, once she had inquired about my health, boyfriend status—I'm divorced—and my career advancement or lack thereof." Sarah smiled. "After all that, I would be treated to discussions about the global food crisis, why agribusiness couldn't meet the demand, and why she refused to sell foods treated with pesticides. She admitted organic farming was less efficient. A lot of goods are lost to bugs and stuff. You didn't so much talk with my late aunt as you listened."

Both Rick and Cooper smiled before Cooper spoke up. "Did your aunt ever talk about what she was reading? That's a gorgeous library. All those books from the nineteenth century and the early twentieth. She must have loved reading or at least collecting."

"Much of that library she inherited, but she was an avid reader. Often she read in French, especially plays and novels. We would laugh about something she quoted from Molière. But mostly, with me, anyway, she would talk about something she'd read in English about farming or about human impact on wildlife."

"It's funny, Miss Price," said Cooper. "I have stopped at your aunt's roadside stand for years and I never knew she could read in French, never knew she owned such beautiful things." She looked around the kitchen, her eyes resting on the old wooden cupboards.

"That doesn't surprise me. I don't know as I would classify Aunt Hester as secretive so much as, uh, compartmentalized." She leaned to her left, toward Rick. "Her friends and interests fell into categories, which didn't overlap."

"Did she talk about them with you?" Rick inquired.

"Not much. Most of what I knew came from my dad, who died about six years ago from lung cancer. He was older than Hester by two years. They got along but weren't close. Too different."

"How?" Cooper often found that an offhand comment, a recollection, pointed in the right direction.

"Oh, Dad was sophisticated, driven. And social. Houston is a great city in which to be social. He married very well. Both my parents loved fine things, evening-gown parties. You know the type. Aunt Hester thought he was superficial."

"Was he?" Rick's eyebrows lifted.

A silence followed this. "By Virginia standards, he was. He talked about money too openly. His suits were too flashy and he wore a big gold Rolex, which Aunt Hester called a Texas timepiece. But Daddy had a heart of gold, so if he wanted to wear a little gold, okay. He made sure I got the best education possible. He went to Houston to make money and he did. Sure, he indulged Mother and he indulged me, but he also made sure I knew right from wrong, and he could be tough. Can you tell? I loved my dad."

"He sounds like a good fellow." Rick nodded. "And Virginians can be snobs. Aunt Hester might have filled those shoes."

"Oh, she didn't mean anything by it. Dad took it with a grain of salt. He called her the Old Maid and declared if she'd find a good man she'd be much less judgmental. I remember Aunt H, as I would call her, used to say to my mother, 'He's my brother, I love him, but how can you live with him?' Mom would laugh."

"What did you think?" Cooper shrewdly asked.

"I guess in some ways I agreed with Dad, but you never got the full picture with Aunt H. Her interests were passionate but compartmentalized, as I said. Like the fishing, for instance. She rarely talked to me about it but she would talk about it for hours to Mom, who liked to fish, too. Once they went together to the Snake River in Wyoming. Dad paid for everything. Aunt Hester was appalled that Mother put on makeup to fish." Sarah laughed, a tinkling, engaging laugh.

"Maybe the fish liked it." Rick laughed with her.

"They must have, because Mom caught more than Aunt H, and that didn't sit well."

"Do you know if she traveled to other places?" Cooper kept on.

"I do know, again through Mom, that Aunt Hester usually fished in Bath or Highland County in Virginia. They both swore it was the best fishing on the East Coast."

"I've heard that," Cooper said. "Do you fish?"

"No. I'm a golfer. Love being out there surrounded by such green vistas, sometimes all by myself. Other times in a foursome. Houston has some wonderful courses. Of course, Charlottesville, for such a small place, does, too."

"Farmington?" Rick raised his voice as a question.

"Those long fairways. Keswick Club is a challenge. Glenmore. A short drive to the Country Club of Virginia. And in four hours I can drive down to Pinehurst, North Carolina, to one of the most fabled golf courses in the country."

"Did Hester golf?" Cooper pressed on.

"No. Her interests were, as you know, varied: fishing, farming, the library, old buildings. She loved the Library of Virginia in Richmond. Loved Monument Avenue. She had a quiet, long-standing interest in the Virginia tribes."

Cooper sat up straighter. "Why do you think she was interested in Virginia Indians?"

"Our maternal line is Sessoms, a Cherokee name," Sarah explained. "But they adapted so well to the early colonists—I mean early as in eighteenth century—that the Sessoms farmed, wore English clothing, spoke English, and intermarried with Europeans. Over time they became so much like the English that they didn't have the trouble the other tribes did, including the Cherokees in the more southern states. Those people went through hell. Sessoms is a common last name in the tribe, just like Adams is a common last name for the Upper Mattaponi."

"Did you know that Josh Hill was an Upper Mattaponi?" Cooper felt that little buzz when she knew she was finding her way on a case.

Where it was going, she didn't know.

Sarah shook her head. "I knew nothing about this fellow, but he appears to have been a fishing buddy, and if he was a member of a Virginia tribe, Aunt H would have been fascinated."

"She never spoke to you about this? About the Cherokee connection?"

"No. It was Dad who told me about that part of our ancestry." She thought a moment. "Once I mentioned something about a bracelet I saw that had been made by the Pueblos. Aunt H said southwestern Indians, Texas Indians, were much different from the East Coast tribes but all were fascinating to study."

"Anything else?" Cooper persisted.

"She said—and this I do remember, because I heard it at odd times, not a lot but enough to remember, and I heard it repeated by my dad, too—the Indians never raped the land."

Both sheriff and deputy sat quietly for a moment, then Rick asked, "Were either of your parents ever involved in environmental causes or perhaps trying to return tribal lands to their original owners?"

"They supported the Nature Conservancy. They made vacations to go on field trips, wonderful places like southern Chile, Moosehead Lake in Maine. They really pitched in with the Nature Conservancy and Ducks Unlimited. We had to live in the now. Mom and Dad wholeheartedly believed that. Dad said that he thought in some ways Aunt H lived too much in the past."

"And Aunt Hester's attitude?" Cooper asked.

"That we needed to make amends. We needed to preserve the past and also make amends to other peoples, to wildlife. As you see, she preserved the past in this house. Aunt H was consistent and she really did care about providing good food at her stand, about taking care of the land. Maybe that's why she liked fishing. She could get away but still be part of nature. I suspect she threw back whatever she caught. Mom always did."

Both interrogators smiled.

Cooper then said, "We combed her roadside stand. Lolly—you met Lolly?" When Sarah nodded yes, Cooper continued. "Showed us the back rooms, everything. She opened the cash register, lifted the tray where Hester kept notes, odd returned checks, stuff like that."

Sarah quietly interrupted, "And you found that my aunt Hester was organized about everything but her financial records. I've found old bank statements in kitchen drawers, in the visor of her truck."

Cooper smiled. "She appears to have used a system unique to herself. What interested us was a check for a thousand dollars written to Joshua Hill. Written on the bottom memo line was 'Research.' It had been cashed."

Sarah registered surprise. "She wouldn't write a check that size on a whim."

"We don't know what the research was, and his records are sparse," Rick said.

"So there is a connection between the murders." Sarah spoke lowly.

"It certainly seems possible," Cooper answered.

"May I ask you a question?" said Sarah.

"Anything." Rick liked her, obviously.

"Do you have any idea who would kill my aunt, or why?"

"I won't b.s. you," he answered. "We don't but I promise you, Sarah, we will find out and we will bring them to justice. Your aunt was a good woman."

Cooper looked Sarah in the eye. "I apologize for pushing you with questions, but you knew Hester as well as anyone, perhaps better. The rest of us took her at face value, and even those who had been in her home, like Mim Sanburne, only knew a fraction of who and what she was."

"You don't think she was involved in anything illegal, do you?" asked Sarah, distressed. "I mean, I can't imagine her doing something illegal. Aunt H was a straight arrow."

"No. But my hunch, and it is just a hunch, is she may have stumbled onto something someone else was doing that was illegal."

Sarah's hand covered her heart for a moment.

"I wonder if she knew she was in danger. She would have kept it to herself. She was so independent, had lived her whole life alone—if she did think she was in danger, she would have thought she could handle it." Sarah swallowed. "I make her sound unrealistic but who could have foreseen something like this? Aunt H never did understand evil."

20

The wind rustled through the dried cornstalks in Buddy Janss's one hundred acres behind the three abandoned schoolhouses. Buddy walked through the fields with an insurance agent. The crop insurer, on overload thanks to the drought, worked every day but Sunday. This Friday, October 25, he had already visited three farms before noon.

The U.S. government underpinned about sixty percent of insurance premiums. Until now, the premiums farmers paid for various farming insurance had more than covered the payouts, but this year it looked as though the government payouts would be greater than the intake.

Looking down at his clipboard, Drake Stoneman, thirty-two, traced acreage numbers with his index finger. "Why do you insure some acres and not others for the same crop?"

Buddy, fifty-two, didn't much like the tone of this younger man nor the assumption, so prevalent these days, that one must explain one's self exhaustively. "Because for years I carted some vegetables and corn to a roadside food stand where the owner was fierce about organic foods."

"Given the losses to fungus, birds, and insects, you must have gotten top dollar." Stoneman looked up from his figures into Buddy's dark brown eyes.

"I did not," the large man replied firmly. "I did business with the lady who owned the stand and my father did business with her people. It's just something I did."

"Hard to farm if you don't put profit first," the college-educated fellow smugly said.

"You don't have much of a life if profit is all you care about." Buddy, feeling his anger rise, then followed with, "I make enough money elsewhere."

Stoneman nodded at the equipment parked nearby. "This your boom sprayer?"

"Is. It's calibrated for each nozzle to spray 1/128 of an acre. Been doing this all my life. Divide the tank capacity by the gallons per acre pesticide or liquid fertilizer application rate. Do the math. Set your nozzles correctly given the crop, figure your normal spraying speed, and record the travel time in seconds. It's the only way to get the application correct. Otherwise, I waste my money."

Drake looked at Buddy, slowly realizing it might be prudent not to lecture him on broadcast applications. "I see."

"You asked about my organic corn, which is how I think of it," said Buddy. "Silver Queen is in this field. As you are a bright fellow from Virginia Tech . . . ?"

Quickly Drake replied, "North Carolina State."

"Uh-huh. You know Silver Queen is hard to grow."

"That I do."

"My untreated acres did better than this one hundred. Look. Lost everything and I sprayed this patch every two days. In this climate, an insect like the corn borer can span three generations in one crop cycle." He yanked an ear off the stalk. "No corn borers."

Just to prove he was on the ball, Drake twisted off an ear himself, separate from the one in Buddy's hand, and inspected it. "I see."

"This entire crop is worthless. Couldn't even use it for forage."

Drake couldn't miss the nasty signs of smut on the now dried-up ears. "It is possible to be fooled. This stuff sometimes just seems to appear overnight."

"I kept after these acres. I shouldn't have any disease in here, including the smut. I sprayed for that, too. I mean, I did everything. Sure, I want my crop insurance. That's why I pay the premiums, but I want to know how this happened."

"I would, too." Drake was becoming a little more sympathetic. "Corn means big bucks. Our country's exports for fresh corn alone, not counting frozen or canned corn, should bring in about $47 million for farmers, and this year it's nowhere close."

"Got to cut growing forty percent of the crop for ethanol when people go hungry," Buddy firmly stated.

"That's a hot potato, Mr. Janss." He paused. "Do you mind if I look at your acres, the ones you used for the roadside stand?"

"Not at all. Everything's off of them."

"Plow under the stalks?"

"No, I leave stuff up until the first hint of spring. Gleanings for birds, bunnies, foxes. Brings 'em right in."

"Why don't you plow this under now so it can start breaking down?"

Buddy wondered what this kid had learned in college.

He calmly explained, "Smut spores can live in the soil, for one. But we do share the earth and the old corn helps wildlife. If I plow it under, the soil will compact by spring and I'll have to break it up again—duplication of effort, hours, and cost, plus I just may have made it easy for the smut to regenerate."

"Uh, yes."

"A ripper and shredder, John Deere 2720, can just tear this up, save time, do a terrific job. But a seventeen-foot with forty disc blades costs almost fifty thousand dollars. The twenty-seven-foot with sixty-six disc blades starts at eighty-nine thousand dollars. Can't begin to afford that. I use my old disc—well, it's ancient, really, and sometimes I even pull my old York rake when the stubble's down. I can't just figure crop profit. I have to factor in equipment costs, hours, wear and tear, and then there's wear and tear on me, too."

Drake knelt down, pulled out a little brown paper bag and a small sharp trowel from his pocket. He dug out a sample of soil. He then walked twenty-five yards, took another one.

Buddy watched. He took his own soil samples each fall and then again in the spring. In this part of the world, a farmer needed to keep checking for magnesium deficiency. Out west the lack was often selenium, not a problem in central Virginia.

Drake came back, Buddy hopped in his new Ford while Drake followed in a serviceable old Ram.

They reached the harvested fields, where the younger man again took soil samples.

Buddy watched, his anger somewhat subsiding. "I can send you my soil tests for all my acres. I'll shoot it to you from my computer."

"That would be helpful. You'll receive your check. Like you said, Mr. Janss, that's why you pay the premiums, and your taxes, too. We need the government for a lot of this. You can imagine the stress on farmers in the Midwest and the Southwest."

"I pray for those people." Buddy meant it, too.

Drake shook his head. "Don't see how people can argue with climate change."

"Actually, Mr. Stoneman, I do see how they can and I have some real questions about our ability to predict and plan how to handle Mother Earth, but I know something's changing. I just want to know more and I'd sure like the politics to be taken out of it."

For a flash Drake dropped his professional mask. "Politics is in everything."

Buddy looked right into his eyes. "You got that right, brother."

As Drake drove away, Buddy folded his arms across his chest, looking over some of his well-tended acreage. It was odd that the untreated Silver Queen corn had done better this year than the treated. He never planted more than two hundred acres with this type of corn, mostly because it took so much management. It was susceptible to about every pest and problem known to corn and needed steady water, too. But, oh, how sweet that Silver Queen was and how people looked forward to it come August, September, and this year, even early October.

Every now and then Buddy would think he'd just plant every field with orchard grass and the hell with it. But he couldn't. He loved his corn crops, loved the squash, and *really* loved the small orchard he tended of the old Alberta pears. People would come from all around to get those pears, not much seen anymore.

Sighing, he stepped on the running board and got into the Ford's cab. He drove back to the disease-ridden crop, parked at the three schoolhouses, and looked for a moment, then drove into the middle of the field.

Harry, pets along with her, happened to be cruising by at that moment to double-check the Halloween Hayride route that Tazio had given her.

She saw Buddy. So she drove out to the field, her old 1978 Ford churning through the hardened, bumpy earth with ease.

As she opened the door, the dog and two cats shot out.

"Buddy. Hey. Saw you here and wanted to thank you again for serving at Hester's house and, well, for being a pallbearer."

"It was an honor to be a pallbearer. Something hits you when you hoist that coffin on your shoulders along with five other men. Can't explain it."

"Well, thank you for honoring a special person."

He leaned against his truck, having stepped out since she left her truck. "Here's something funny goin' on. Wish Hester were with us, she'd crow with delight. These acres, sprayed every two days. My Silver Queen. Well, smut ruined everything. The untreated Silver Queen acres—healthy. Oh, sure, a worm here and there, and always corn spiders, but they do no harm. The birds got some of the corn, but mostly my untreated acres are really healthy, even with our brief drought. I can't figure it out."

"What about your irrigated acres?"

"Same story. I irrigated half my plots. The irrigated rows did a little better but not as much as one would think, but, you know"—he swept his hand westward—"so many creeks, and I think some of that moisture in the air from them helped. But like I said to you before, my crop yield varied from one side of the road to the other, but this, this is smut and I don't know what's going on. I read all the time and I haven't read anywhere where smut has become resistant to treatment. Now, we know some insects are becoming resistant. I'll get my insurance check but I want to figure this out. I'm here to grow good crops, not to collect money for failure."

"I hear you." Harry studied the midsized John Deere tractor parked fifty yards off, boom on the back. "Mind if I look? I'd love to get a boom and I'd sure love to get a drill seeder, too."

"I'll tell you if I see anything used that's in good shape. Stuff new costs as much as a car or a house these days."

"Yeah, I know."

They reached the green and yellow tractor. It had a tank affixed to the back, with a long boom off that. "I used to rely on a gravity

feed, but now I've got a small pump to suck out any stuff on the bottom," Buddy told her.

"You thought of everything." Harry admired practical solutions.

He smiled. "Try. I need to flush this baby out and take her back to the shed for the winter. You know, Harry, I kind of lost heart. Since I pulled down that first husk and saw the damage, I haven't done much in here."

Tucker, right under the machine's tank, called out, "*No chemicals. Can't smell a one. What's he spraying with?*"

The two cats joined her.

Pewter sniffed. "*Smells, though.*"

"*Does,*" Mrs. Murphy agreed, then jumped on the back of the boom hitch and up onto the tank, where she balanced herself and tapped at the screw-on cap.

Harry laughed. "Looks like we've got a Future Farmer of America here."

"*Open it up. Come on. There's no chemicals in here. We'd know,*" the cat pleaded.

Smiling, Harry did untwist the cap as Mrs. Murphy jumped off. Harry peered into the tank. "Buddy," she said, sniffing, "Buddy, look at this."

He dutifully did and immediately became enraged at the sight. "Goddammit to hell!" Then he apologized. "Sorry."

"Buddy, I'd have said worse."

The tank had smut in the bottom. With his own system, Buddy had infected his crop.

"Harry, I calibrated the gallons per acre. I flushed the system clean, I checked every screw, nozzle, everything. And I refilled this tank each morning."

"Well, Buddy, someone drained your tank halfway, put a smut slurry in, then refilled it. How would you know? And I bet they cleaned it after you left the day's work. Someone who knows farming also knows your schedule. And smut spores are easy to grow. You can do it in your kitchen."

His face blanched, then turned scarlet. "Why? Who would do such a thing?" He paused, color deepening. "I'll kill the S.O.B."

Harry said nothing. Any talk of killing right now gave her a chill.

21

Adjustable wrench in hand, Fair frowned as he worked in the big red shed near the barn. "That's strange," he said, squinting at the dismantled ATV in front of him.

"Honey, there's so much weird stuff going on around here, this is just one more thing, but to deliberately put smut in a spray tank . . ." Harry shook her head. "Why?"

"You don't think it could have occurred naturally?"

"No."

"Well, it will all come out in the wash." He checked the sun, now low in the sky above the fields. "I'd better start putting this back together."

"Did you find the problem?"

"The first problem was the fuel line clogged. The second problem—I'm not sure but this generator isn't going off."

Harry peered down into the ATV's engine. "It's a bitty thing."

"Anything compared to the engine in your '78 Ford is a bitty thing. Well, let me put this back together. We need it."

"If we can't get it back working, I'll call Wayne's Cycle." She mentioned the place where they had bought the ATV years back in Waynesboro, then realized her husband didn't want to hear that.

RITA MAE BROWN & SNEAKY PIE BROWN

"It will run," he loudly announced.

As she walked back to the house, Tucker beside her, she looked over her fields, the sunflowers all harvested. "Time to plow stuff under," she said to the corgi.

"*If you leave it alone, rabbits will come in,*" Tucker said. She liked to chase rabbits.

Pushing open the screen door, Harry heard a frantic scramble on the kitchen countertops.

"*You forgot to completely close the toaster oven,*" said the corgi. "*I smell the corn bread.*"

Stepping into the kitchen, no cats in sight, Harry noticed corn bread crumbs strewn across the counter in front of the toaster oven.

"Those boogers!"

The cats had hooked the corn bread inside the toaster oven, tearing pieces off, pulling them out of the oven and onto the counter, where they ate them. However, they had been interrupted in their thievery, so crumbles—golden evidence—lay scattered on the counter and on the floor.

Since some was on the floor, Tucker ate it. No point in letting food go to waste.

Before Harry could cuss, the phone rang.

"Susan," Harry greeted her.

"I got a job," came her enthusiastic voice.

"Where?"

"At Ivy Nurseries. I'll be making arrangements and stuff like that."

"Wonderful."

"Well, I learned a lot from you."

"You learned more from Miranda."

Miranda Hogendobber, a passionate gardener and former coworker at the post office, possessed a gift for arranging height,

146

color, breadth. If it involved a flower, Miranda could grow it, then display it.

Susan replied warmly, "How about I give you both credit? I need to do more than I've been doing."

Harry then told her about the corn smut and Buddy. "Never saw him so mad."

"Remind me, what's corn smut?"

"It's a fungus. It can survive during the winter if it finds the right place to hide. It can survive in old cornstalks, but usually the wind has blown spores all over the place after the swollen infected kernels explode. Not a lot left in the stalks. You and I could grow smut ourselves in corn. The later-maturing corn varieties are more susceptible to it. Has a lot to do with the change in nighttime temperature from midsummer. And when kernels explode, you can see the stuff. It's actually not that hard to control if you spray before you get it. Once you get it, though, you might as well forget it, and sweet corn is pretty vulnerable."

"Doesn't make sense."

"No, it doesn't. Before I forget, when do you start your job?"

"Monday."

"I'll drop by the nursery around quitting time."

"Great."

They hung up. Harry looked out the window over the sink. She could tell from her husband's walk that he hadn't fixed the ATV. She wouldn't bring it up but she would make sure the magnetic card for Wayne's Cycle was moved to the front of the refrigerator.

Given the scowl on his face, she thought she'd better distract him. She disappeared into the small workroom and turned on the computer.

Mrs. Murphy and Pewter smelled the computer. Humans couldn't detect the smell computers gave off when they were working, but for the cats the odor was coppery, distinctive.

"*She gets wrapped up with that nonsense,*" Pewter gloated. "*She'll forget what we did.*"

"*She won't forget but she will be occupied. That corn bread, oh, full of butter.*" Mrs. Murphy smiled.

The two cats wiggled out from under the bed where they'd been hiding and silently made their way into Fair's small office, where Harry peered at the screen.

Fair, calmer now, stuck his head in. "What's cooking?"

"Lasagna," answered Harry.

"No, I mean, what's cooking here?" He pointed to the computer.

"*Lasagna,*" Pewter said, sounding crushed. "*Not my favorite but it's okay.*"

"*You'll eat. You'll eat anything,*" said Mrs. Murphy.

The culprits tiptoed to one side of the desk, sitting to listen.

"I'm looking up corn stuff," Harry explained to her husband. "Like, did you know that people living in what is now Mexico domesticated corn fourteen thousand years ago?"

"Isn't corn basically a grass crop?"

"Yeah, but says here that the original plant didn't look anything like modern corn. They called it *teosinte*."

He stood next to her now. "Fourteen thousand years ago. Imagine if you got a toothache back then. Ouch."

"Hurts enough now." She looked up at him, then back at the screen.

"Says here that what we call sweet corn was first grown in Pennsylvania in the mid-1700s. The first commercial variety was introduced in 1779." She scrolled up more stuff. "Hey, hey, honey, how about this?"

He leaned down and read along with her. "Corn invaded by corn smut is considered a delicacy in Mexico. Infested corn was cooked even before Columbus."

"Guess every culture enjoys its delicacies." She touched his hand. "But maybe Buddy can make a little money. I'm going to call him."

"Okay. I'll shower."

"Thirty minutes to supper at the most."

He kissed her on the cheek.

She dialed Buddy Janss, launched right in with her discovery.

"They eat that stuff?" replied an incredulous Buddy.

"Buddy, if you go to your computer, Metapathogen.com has a little section on corn smut, under its Latin name, *Ustilago maydis*. Yeah, Mexican restaurants think it's terrific."

"Well, I already walked the insurance agent through."

"You did, but if you call around to some really fancy Mexican restaurants, maybe you can figure prices. Obviously, if they'll pay more than the crop insurance, that's an easy decision."

"You bet." His voice picked up energy.

"Before it slips my mind, when Cooper and I walked through Hester's library looking at her beautiful books, we found some on fishing, and a picture of her with a friend fishing. She ever talk about this with you?" Harry pointedly did not mention the friend was scarecrow Josh Hill.

"Oh, well now, over the years maybe once or twice. Hester and I mostly stuck to business." He chuckled. "Her version of business."

"Had you ever been in her house before the reception?"

"No. What about you?"

"Me neither. I was surprised at how lovely it was. And the expensive things she owned."

"Life is full of surprises."

22

*S*aturdays Harry and Fair liked to join their friends for foxhunting. As the fox was chased, not killed, they especially enjoyed riding behind hounds, land rolling before them like green waves, Blue Ridge Mountains behind, a splendid theatrical backdrop.

Today's hunt lasted three hours. Once back at their trailers, people wiped down horses and threw sweat sheets over them, since it was warm, in the mid-fifties. After putting out buckets of water, they hurried to join everyone else at the tailgate. Literally it was a tailgate: The tailgates on trucks were dropped, a few card tables were put out and little oil tablecloths were tossed over them.

The talk always began with the day's sport before rapidly moving to other subjects. Many of today's hunters had also attended Hester's service.

Big Mim, hot coffee in hand, mentioned, "I believe Sarah Price will take over Hester's house."

"Wonderful," Wesley said, nodding.

"I'd think you'd feel otherwise," said Neil with a hint of sarcasm. He was a non-rider who'd come to join the group, as did others, food and drink being a reliable magnet.

"Why? It's a piece of old Virginia, and better that such places stay in the family."

"Ah." Neil swilled his scotch. "You're right. I was thinking of the commission on a sale. Would sell for a lot, that place."

Harry said, "I couldn't possibly afford my farm today. It's kind of crazy."

"Prices go up and down," said Wesley, "but when it comes to beautiful farms in Virginia, they have held steady despite all. Now, I'm not saying I've sold a lot lately, mind you, but we are in a better position than most of the country."

"Not the boom towns," Neil pressed.

"Like Oklahoma City?" Fair asked. "You know, it's exciting when something hits like the boom in the Dakotas and Oklahoma. Hope, energy, jobs, but you wonder how it will all turn out down the road."

"Honey, that's true for everything." Harry smiled, then focused on Neil. "How about fertilizer samples? Just enough to, say, put on three small patches, four feet by four feet. I'll make little squares back behind the sunflowers."

"Be happy to. I know if you have a good experience and endorse my products, others will follow." Neil was right about that. "Have you thought about what you would be growing?"

"Have."

Tazio and her boyfriend, Paul Diaz, joined them. As Paul rode and trained Big Mim's horses, Tazio had realized she'd better learn to ride.

To Paul's credit, he was studying architecture, and the two, on his weekday off, would drive to Richmond, Washington, and other places to look at buildings constructed at different periods in our history. He found he liked it, just as Tazio found she liked riding.

"She's going to move up to Second Flight," Paul bragged of Tazio, referring to the foxhunting group closer to the action.

Tazio rode in the back on an adorable babysitter of a horse, but as she gained skill and confidence, she would move up a notch.

"Never doubted that for a minute," Fair told her.

"How's it coming for the Halloween Hayride?" Neil asked.

"Frankenstein will be ready," said Tazio. "He'll snap the restraining belts, climb off the table, attack the good doctor"—she nodded at Wesley—"then run out the door."

"I'm scared already," Harry said.

Neil laughed. "It's going to be the scariest hayride ever, and we will raise a bundle. I'm committed to that and others are, too."

"I think a room in the library should be named for Hester," Harry thought out loud.

"You're right, honey," Fair agreed.

"After the hayride, we can bring it before the library board. I'm getting excited about this." Neil smiled.

"You get excited about anything that makes money," Wesley teased him.

"Profit motive. Built this country," Neil fired back.

Big Mim, who had left the group, sailed back into their conversation, changing the subject. "Given the dryness, not a bad hunt. We do need rain, though. Desperately."

"That we do," Fair said. "The ground is so hard it's like running on brick."

"Tazio," Big Mim addressed the architect, who looked stunning in hunt kit, "you've been over there at the school buildings. Are they salvageable?"

With a big grin, Tazio replied, "They are in great shape. The real expense in fixing them up would be plumbing, heating, air-conditioning. But those buildings were solidly built, well sited, and there's not even a leak in those roofs. You could actually still use the huge cast-iron furnaces."

"Good," Big Mim said. "Lot of history there."

"I wish older people would write down what they lived through—the good, the bad, and the ugly," Harry said with some emotion. "History books can be dry or filled with speculation about this world force and that armament technology. I want to hear what people who lived through it all thought and felt."

"Good point." Tazio rested her hand on Harry's shoulder for a moment.

"Speaking of knowing, the TV reporters and the newspaper say that Hester was shot," said Neil. "And so was that fellow you found in the Morrowdale field. But how and where were they shot, exactly?" he asked, not realizing that Harry might not wish to recall any of this.

"I don't know," she replied.

Fair stepped in. "When we found the scarecrow, he was fully dressed. Hester was, too. No wounds were evident."

"Neil, I don't really *want* to know," Harry lied. Cooper had told her they were shot through the heart. Cooper had also told her the sheriff's department was withholding the exact M.O. "They're both gone, a young man and a neighbor. That's enough."

Neil shrugged. "I guess I get too curious. Too many crime shows on television."

"It's always so antiseptic, those shows. No faces frozen in horror." Tazio reached for Paul's hand. "What I want to know is why our society is so enthralled by crime and violence. Why can't we be enthralled by beauty, harmony, or perfect proportion?"

"Because they demand sensitivity." Fair surprised them by coming right out with this. "Anyone can see a beautiful sunrise or hear great music, but not everyone can *feel* it. Yet everyone can feel violence."

"I never thought of that," Wesley remarked.

"And I suppose everyone can kill," Tazio said, "but how many people can compose a symphony?"

"I'm not sure everyone can kill," Neil replied. "Then again, I don't want to find out."

To change the subject, Harry asked Tazio, "That old slip of paper you found—did you by any chance check to see if it was a student? I mean, I wonder if they have the old rolls."

"I didn't find out yet."

"What was the name?" Wesley was nosy.

"Walter Ashby Plecker," Tazio answered.

23

Later that afternoon, after Harry finished her barn chores, she set up shop at the computer in the tack room. Outside, the sun was already setting as Simon, the possum, peeped over the hayloft.

Patrolling the barn's center aisle while the horses munched away, Mrs. Murphy heard the possum's squeak.

"Murphy?"

"What, Simon?"

"What does she do in there? I see that bluish light. She sits there for hours! It's unnatural for people to sit still that long."

"Ha." Pewter, faking her patrol, stopped to look up. "Millions of people sit on their butts for weeks and years. After a while, part of them is in the next zip code."

"Look who's talking," sassed Tucker, plonked down on an aisle tack trunk.

For a fat girl, Pewter could move. She flew down the aisle, jumped onto the tack trunk, batted the corgi with an extended claw, then leapt off in an attempt to flee the barn, Tucker in pursuit.

"I loathe violence." Simon closed his eyes.

"Mmm," was the tiger cat's reply, since she often considered bat-

ting Pewter, as well as Tucker. Well, more Pewter than Tucker—she could reason with Tucker.

Heavyset though she was, Pewter easily flummoxed the dog. She could zig and zag so quickly that Tucker would skid out trying to catch her. Then Pewter would run straightaway, Tucker would make up lost ground, and once again the cat would turn. She even stopped dead in her tracks, faced the onrushing dog, then soared right over Tucker, who by now was barking nonstop.

"I hate you!" barked the corgi. "I really, really hate you."

"Peon!" Pewter gleefully tormented the dog.

"What now?" Hearing the clamor, Harry pushed away from the computer and walked outside. "All right, you two. Calm down."

"Kill. I want to kill!" Tucker practically foamed at the mouth.

"Bubble Butt, Tailless Wonder!" Pewter was merciless as she climbed a gum tree, then spread out on a lower branch like a courtesan, tail swaying to and fro. "You'll never catch me," she taunted.

"You have to sleep sometime." Tucker stood on her hind legs, reaching as high as she could with her front paws on the thick ridged bark.

"I sleep with one eye open," Pewter called down in a singsong voice.

"What a liar she is," laughed Mrs. Murphy, now with the human.

Grabbing Tucker by her rolled leather collar, Harry pulled the enraged dog away from the tree. Pewter watched from above, enjoying the spectacle.

"Tucker, leave it," Harry ordered.

"Really, Tucker," Mrs. Murphy counseled. "She's not worth this much emotion."

Tucker stared imploringly at Harry. "You don't know how awful she is. You don't know how I suffer." She thought a moment, searching for further damning ideas. "I think she's a member of a Confederate underground. She's gray, you know. She wants to restore the old ways. She's really, really awful."

Mrs. Murphy laughed, while poor Simon, who had run to view this chase from the opened upper hayloft door, wrung his front paws. "*Tucker, she would be the same no matter if it was the old days or these days,*" he said.

"*She'd be worse. I know it.*" Tucker still stared at Harry, who reached down to pat her silky head.

As though singing an aria, Pewter meowed, "*She can dish it out but she can't take it.*"

"Pewter, that's the worst screeching ever," Harry insulted the cat. "Now, here's the deal. If you don't behave, it's lockdown. Separate rooms. Closed doors. No treats. Hear that? No treats."

Tucker growled low. "*I'd starve to get even.*"

"*I wouldn't.*" Pewter hastily backed down the tree, circled Tucker so she would be behind Harry, then rubbed the human's legs while purring mightily.

"*How can she fall for this?*" Crestfallen, Tucker lowered her head.

"*Because she likes me better.*" Pewter kept rubbing.

"I can't concentrate when you all carry on like this," Harry complained. "Too much noise. If we were in the house, God only knows what would have been smashed to bits. Now come on. Settle down." She turned to go back to the barn.

Dutifully, Tucker stuck by the human's heels while Pewter, in a flash of glory, or so she thought, raced ahead, tail straight up. She paused for a moment, then Mrs. Murphy zoomed up next to her and the two cats chased each other, in good fun, to the barn.

Harry loved watching animals play. "Tucker, cats are, well, cats. They'll chase each other, play-hiss, howl—it's just dumb stuff. You, being a sober and responsible dog, are above it."

Tucker considered this and thought for a fraction of a moment that maybe Harry did understand. To some extent, she did. Anyone who lives with cats figures out soon enough they will do what they want.

Back in her tack room chair, Harry wiggled to get comfortable. The lamp she was using until she could buy the Italian light bulb—which is how she thought of it—couldn't shine its light as precisely as the designer one, but it was okay.

Tucker flopped at her feet. This made Harry happy because she always enjoyed reporting her progress to the dog, who invariably perked her ears at Harry's voice.

"Tucker, I have gotten into the county records for students, but the records for Random Row are spotty at best. I'm trying to find a student's name that was on a piece of paper in the teacher's desk." She scrolled through the years. "The years before 1918 aren't even entered. They microfilmed the written records back in the 1960s. Maybe the handwritten records are in a forgotten vault somewhere in the county building." She kept clicking the mouse. "Oh, hey, they actually scanned them in. The handwriting is beautiful. I can't make some of this out, but there does not appear to be a student named Walter Ashby Plecker."

Missing his wife, Fair walked into the barn, looked up, and saw Simon. "Hey, fella."

"Hey," said Simon, then scuttled away.

Fair entered the tack room. "Simon is such a scaredy-cat. 'Course, most possums are."

"It helps if you feed him." Harry leaned her chin on her hand. "Molasses on bread or molasses in the snow."

"I know, but when am I going to have time to feed a possum? When do you have time?"

She smiled up at him. "I do it every day."

"*Feeds us, too,*" Shortro, the athletic Saddlebred horse in the stall next to the tack room, called out.

Tomahawk, Harry's beloved Thoroughbred, also nickered. "*We love Harry,*" he declared.

All the horses agreed, and up in his nest even Simon squeaked, "*Me, too.*"

The two cats entered the tack room just as Harry finished telling Fair about her failure to find any information on the mysterious name.

"Here." He leaned over, typed a bit, then stood back. "You did the logical thing. You assumed Walter was a student's name because the paper was found in the teacher's desk. I just punched in his name to see what would show up. There you go." Fair started to read over her shoulder. "Hmm, not so good," he said.

"Why didn't I think of that?" Harry, delighted that her husband was smart, was equally put out by her own slowness on this subject.

She read along with him. " '*Paper genocide* is often the term used to describe the actions of Walter Ashby Plecker, the government employee who was head of Vital Statistics in Virginia from 1912 to 1946.' "

Fair continued. " 'Plecker replaced the term *Indian* with the term *colored* on all official documents, birth and death certificates, marriage licenses, and voter registration forms.' " He stepped back a moment. "Paper genocide."

She looked up at her husband. "Fair, what does it mean exactly?"

"I'm not sure but I think it means that if everyone is jammed under one umbrella, you can treat or mistreat everyone the same. This is bizarre." He read more as she scrolled down the text. " 'Members of Virginia Indian tribes are severely handicapped in proving they are indeed Indians according to federal standards. They can't apply for scholarships or receive federal funds for housing, health care, or economic development.' " He stopped looking at the screen, looked at his wife. "And, of course, they can't open casinos, which brings in big bucks. Wait a minute, here. Says the Virginia tribes do not want to open casinos and have signed away those rights." He'd returned his gaze to the computer screen.

"Fair, this is a terrible thing." She read more on the subject. "'Seven Virginia governors, irrespective of party affiliation, have supported federal recognition of Virginia's Indians.' But, in so many words, they've been told to sit on a tack."

"Hey, look at this. No Virginia tribe member can return their ancestors' bones to a rightful and respectful burial. Harry, this is outrageous. I mean, I had no idea. This is one of the most disgusting things I have ever read."

"Well," Harry said, "a bill, H.R. 783, the Thomasina E. Jordan Indian Tribes of Virginia Federal Recognition Act of 2011, is presently working its way through Congress. Yeah, right. And how many bills prior to this have died in one subcommittee or another?"

Fair rarely swore but he let it fly. "Bastards."

"Walter Ashby Plecker appears to have been the biggest bastard of the bunch, and it's just rolled on from there." Stunned and deeply disturbed, Harry clicked off her computer. "Let's call Coop," she said, standing.

"Why?"

"Come on. Let's go inside and use the house line. Anything ever spoken on a cellphone is out there somewhere."

Intrigued, he followed his wife into the kitchen, as did the two cats and the dog.

Harry rang Cooper up on the kitchen wall phone and explained what she and Fair had discovered about Walter Ashby Plecker. "It's only a scrap of paper but maybe you should ask Sarah Price if you can go through Hester's desk to see if there's a link. After all, Hester had Cherokee blood on her mother's side, and Josh was a member of the Upper Mattaponi tribe."

"I've asked Sarah to go through Hester's things on Monday, and I'll be there with her."

Urgency in her voice, Harry prodded. "Move it up. Go tomorrow, Sunday, if she'll do it."

"Harry, this isn't much to go on."

"It's a long shot, a really long shot, Cooper, but right now it's one of the few links between the two murders, other than both corpses were dressed for Halloween, cleverly disguised."

A long, long pause followed this. Over the phone line, Harry could almost hear Cooper's mind whirring. "All right."

Husband and wife remained silent after Harry hung up.

Finally, Fair said, "While you were on your computer in the barn, I was on mine. Come on. I have something to show you."

Once inside his small, tidy office, he showed her an article reporting that jobs exposing women to plastics and man-made chemicals greatly elevate a woman's chance of developing breast cancer.

He pointed to the screen. "A long-term study of more than two thousand women in Ontario found those who worked for at least ten years in food canning and automotive plastics developed cancer at a rate five times higher than women in other jobs. Chemicals such as BPA—bisphenol A—are to blame."

She replied, "I'm a farmer. Well, I worked in the post office after college. I've checked out fine at every exam for the last two years, and after my next checkup, I won't have to go back for six months. I'm okay."

Fair, who had felt shocked, frightened, and useless when his wife was diagnosed with stage I breast cancer two years ago, still carried with him the fear that it might return. Because of this, he was vigilant concerning cancer research and treatments. "Read on."

"Pesticide exposure is also elevated for female farm workers." She quieted for a moment. "I rarely use much of anything."

"What about your father?"

She nodded. "He used more. Cut back later on, but he said that in the beginning they thought those things were a godsend."

"Our air, food, and water are loaded with chemicals unheard of even fifty years ago. BPA and phthalates, to name a few, are known hormone disrupters. I see so much more cancer in horses than I did when I started practicing as a vet." Harry's husband looked stricken..

"Honey, my cancer is not coming back," she assured him.

"I know." He kissed her cheek. "But now that you've been through it, I want to keep abreast of recent research, forgive the pun."

They both laughed and she hugged him when he stood up. "You're stuck with me."

"Better be, which reminds me: Carry your father's old snub-nosed .38."

"I can't shoot cancer cells."

"No, but you can't keep your nose out of those two murders. I know you. Just carry the gun."

24

"*A* Montblanc Diplomat," Cooper said the next afternoon, holding up the fancy pen, which she had fetched from the drawer of Hester's desk.

"She didn't have much or spend much, but what she had was the very best." Sarah smiled, remembering her aunt's lectures on prudent expenditures. "If she was going to fork out cash, it had to be for something that would last."

"This certainly will." Cooper studied the gold point. "Medium."

"How do you know so much about pens?"

Cooper laughed. "How do you?"

"Drilled into my head: Write in your own hand on good paper. Always write a thank-you and a condolence, and, of course, the condolence should never be on pastel paper. The rules, but I'm glad I know them. Of course, who in my generation practices such etiquette?"

"We're close in age. I kind of think these things are coming back. I mean good stationery, fountain pens, elegant clothing, and hats for men, too. Cycles. Then again, how many butt cracks can you observe before you decide that maybe low-rise trousers are not the way to go?"

Sarah, emitting peals of laughter, snatched a heavy wooden ruler from the desk. "This would solve a lot of problems in that regard."

Cooper laughed, too, as they both kept rooting through the long drawer of the antique desk.

Sarah pulled out a Smythson leather-bound day calendar. "Probably you should keep this, and take a lot of time with it."

"Right." Cooper ran her forefinger over the textured leather. "I don't see a computer anywhere in here."

"Aunt H didn't have one at home, just one at the stand, which you know about. I'd bug her about it but she said when she came home she didn't want to think about work."

"We've already got someone working on the store computer with Lolly. Lolly still needs it to transact business. Working in the evening, our computer whiz found sales, purchases, and a soil map for Albemarle County with the farms she did business with clearly marked. Wherever she bought anything from anyone, she checked their soils. She really was a very thorough person."

"About most everything. Dad was that way, too. 'If you're going to do it, do it right.' Must have heard that a thousand times." Sarah sighed and smiled. "I miss them. I will miss their generation and my grandparents' generation. I never really thought about it much before." She blinked. "Sorry. You're here to go through Aunt H's effects and I'm babbling on."

"Not babble. It does kind of dawn on you that nobody is here forever. Then you have to realize you won't be here forever either. I see enough death in my line of work to give me great respect for life."

Sarah tilted her head. "Officer, that's a wonderful thought."

"Will you call me Cooper? I'm not even in uniform. Thank God. I mean, have you ever seen a law enforcement uniform that looked good on a woman?"

"Now that you mention it, there's never quite enough room for . . ." Sarah made a rolling motion over her breasts.

Again they both laughed.

"Nothing here," Cooper said, glancing at an empty drawer. "There's still this big one on the bottom, the double drawer. Let me get on my knees and hand you the files." She did just that.

Sarah arranged the files in neat piles. "Hmm," she said, reading the tabs. "A lot on fertilizer, pesticides, wildlife studies. County soil and water maps."

"Probably hard copies of the maps that are on the work computer." Cooper pulled out the map file, flipped it open, and unfolded a large county map.

Sarah reached into the open folder. "Here's the info key."

Cooper studied the numbers and the outlines, all in different colors. "Number one is her own holdings. Pretty good soil. Number two is eastern Albemarle. Hmm, not as much produce over there. She has most of it marked as hay." Cooper ran her finger back to western Albemarle. "Morrowdale, that's a beautiful farm out on Garth Road, where we found the first body. According to Hester, good soil, but she has the pesticide sign near some of the acres. I guess that means they were sprayed."

"Look at all three yellow outlines. Someone owns a lot of property," Sarah remarked.

Cooper checked the key again. "That's Buddy Janss, the big man who served punch at the reception. He rents most of it."

"He must be rich."

"Land poor might be another way to put it." Cooper smiled. "He owns maybe eight hundred acres outright. Rents the rest, so he has a lot of money sunk into soil improvement. That's the conundrum of renting land. You usually need to improve it. Most landowners, especially suburban or city people who buy in the country, don't want to spend money on their fields and don't realize how important it is. Buddy dutifully fertilizes, weeds, tests soil. He doesn't want to sell his acres if he can help it. And he'd buy what he rents if he could."

"Who is in chartreuse?"

Cooper ran her finger down the list. "Neil Jordan. Hester marked what's owned, what's rented, and what's for sale. She must have updated this weekly."

Cooper folded the map and placed it back in the manila folder, then pulled out the file on fertilizers. "This is full of equations," she exclaimed.

Sarah studied the figures. "Aunt H took high school chemistry. Maybe she took more when she was at Mary Baldwin."

"Bet she did. This stuff is complicated." Cooper shook her head.

"The brochures aren't." Sarah handed her a pile of glossy brochures for fertilizer products, featuring photos of lush fields of corn, wheat, soybeans, even orchard rows.

Cooper examined a pamphlet. "Here's one that Neil Jordan wrote on the back of, telling your aunt to call him if she had questions. It's for a new fertilizer."

"If it was a natural product, she probably did call him, but she was wary, as you know, and she was really opposed to anything petroleum based," said Sarah. "She would say something about it to me every now and then, but not too much since I don't understand agriculture."

"Did she ever ask you about your work?"

"A little. Enough to tell me it's boring, which it is." Sarah looked directly at Cooper. "Insurance is a good thing to have but so much of it is oversold on fears. I've done well, but I, well . . ." She shrugged. "I think I can walk away from it now, thanks to Aunt H."

"She must have loved you very much."

Sarah's eyes teared up, then she laughed her tinkling laugh. "I was her only heir. I suppose she had to love me."

"Big Mim put the word out that you're going to move here. Live in Hester's house. Keep the family place alive. Oh, Big Mim runs Crozet, which I should have told you or someone should have told you before the reception."

"Susan Tucker filled me in on all the locals. I learned who, what, when, and where, and sometimes why. Aunt H, when I'd come on visits, didn't much talk about other people."

Chin on her hand now, Cooper pulled out another folder, flipping it open.

She sat up straighter. "Here are the procedures for officially establishing an American Indian group as an Indian tribe." She read a footnote. "The seven criteria are presented here in abbreviated form. 'For the complete federal text, refer to 25 CFR Part 83.' Huh?"

Sarah rummaged through the files. "She's got some really old stuff here. Stuff before computers took over. It looks to be clearly presented. It's all about the Virginia Indian tribes. What about the criteria you have, is it more recent stuff?"

"Number one is, 'The petitioner has been identified as an American Indian entity on a substantially continuous basis since 1900.'"

"My list says, 'Be identified from historic times until the present on a substantially continuous basis as *American Indian* or *aboriginal*.'"

Each reviewed the other's list and the language.

"Your list is clearer," Sarah said.

"It is. Number two: 'Prove that a substantial portion of members lives in a specific area or lives as a community viewed as American Indian and distinct from other populations of the area;

and prove that members of this community are descendants of an Indian tribe.'"

"That's easy to do in the western states." Sarah read on for Cooper. "Number three: 'Prove that it has maintained tribal political influence or other authority over its members as an autonomous entity throughout history until the present.'"

Cooper read on, then threw up her hands. "All this crap about documentation. If you've been moved around or removed, how can you provide documentation to the very same government that's screwing you?" She stopped herself. "Sorry."

"No, no. I understand, but this is even worse." While flipping through the papers, Sarah had plucked out the criteria needed for an individual to prove he was Indian, as described by the Bureau of Indian Affairs. "This is real betrayal. Worse than 'screwing you.' Look at this."

Cooper read the passage, then said, "This is flat-out impossible. You have to give the maiden names of all women listed on the request for the Certificate of Degree of Indian Blood. So you need, at the least, your mother and grandmother's maiden names. You can abbreviate that to CDIB. How helpful."

Sarah continued in Cooper's line. "Birth certificates? Okay, that's reasonable. 'Delayed birth certificates,' what in the devil does that mean? Death certificates . . . and 'the Indian tribe must have a duly adopted tribal ordinance concerning the issuance of such documents.' So you can't be born or die according to your customs, you have to do it the U.S. government way and prove it? And your degree of Indian blood can only be computed if there are records of ancestors of Indian blood who were listed on an official roll." Sarah caught her breath. "This is a bureaucratic paper nightmare."

"Paper genocide," Cooper whispered.

"What?"

Cooper explained what Harry had told her about Walter Ashby Plecker and the peculiar phrase linked to him.

Sarah was silent for a long time, then said, "It is genocide. Dear God, it is. Why did Aunt H have all this stuff?"

"Do you think she might have wanted to prove her own Cherokee blood?"

"No. There would be no way to prove it and by now it's so intermingled with, for lack of a better description, British Isles blood." Sarah shook her head.

"Yeah." Cooper stared at the folder, then turned more pages. "Obviously, Hester was fascinated with this. And you know about the Virginia tribes not being recognized by the federal government?"

As Sarah did not, Cooper explained. Sarah exploded, "They're totally ripped off. It isn't even the loans and all that stuff. It's needing to be recognized for surviving at all, for keeping their cultural integrity intact. This may sound odd but one of the main reasons I go to Mass is for the liturgy, for the tradition. It's my culture. It has been intact for two thousand years. I am saying and praying what people before me prayed throughout the centuries. I need that. Doesn't it make sense that those of Indian blood need their customs, spiritual solace?"

Cooper returned to the file. "It does make sense. It's more important than the money, but I'm willing to bet the reason this is all so complicated and difficult is the government doesn't want thousands of people applying for scholarships, loans, you name it."

"Everything comes down to money. Like divorce. A relationship devolves into fighting over money and who gets the couch. Pretty much the whole thing repulses me."

"Divorce?" Cooper half-smiled at her.

"Yeah, but what I'm really talking about is bean counting. That's what I do at the insurance company: I count beans."

Cooper took in what the young woman said, then returned her gaze to the file in front of her. "Says here that tribes may purchase or reacquire traditional lands and have the property placed in trust status, exempt from state or county rules, including, in some cases, zoning restrictions." She read more. "This states the possible land base for Virginia Indians is too small here."

"I don't believe that," Sarah said. "It's just that the land has been in other hands for centuries. White folks got here in 1607. Well, earlier if you count the city of St. Augustine down in Florida."

"Here's something else," Cooper said. "If a close affiliation with a property can be shown, the tribe might reclaim the lands or demand damages for its 'illegal' usage—'illegal' is in quotes—many years ago. Means church and school lands used by the Catholic Church, Quakers, etc., could possibly be reclaimed, bought back, and some sort of reparation deal structured."

"What a mess, except it isn't because it's hidden," Sarah said. "Squelched. People nowadays are too busy downloading the latest film to even think about something like this."

Cooper smiled again at Hester's niece. "I don't think being self-centered is unique to our time. We simply have more ways to pursue it." She then looked down before exclaiming, "Big bucks!"

Sarah took the paper from Cooper's hand and read, "'The Mashantucket Pequots of Connecticut run the biggest money-maker in the western hemisphere with their casino.' All the other tribal-owned casinos are listed here with profits. And there's a note at the bottom."

Cooper read out loud: "'Dear Hester, Per your request. It's fascinating. Think of the fly rods one could buy with even a sliver of those profits. Ha. Your buddy, Josh.'"

Cooper's face turned pale. "He was onto something. He had to be. He couldn't have been killed in such a bizarre way for finding an accounting error in the books of the local convenience store."

"Maybe he wanted to push for a casino."

"But the Virginia Indians signed away that possibility."

"Laws can be overturned. It must be something like that, Cooper, because my aunt would never, ever be involved in something underhanded. She wanted just enough to live decently and wished the same for others."

"Sarah, I know that's the truth, but your aunt Hester discovered something dangerous, and I'll bet she shared it with Josh."

25

*B*rilliant sunshine flooded Harry's fields and pastures Monday afternoon, turning golden the sunflower stubble and the plowed fields.

Soil map in hand, Neil Jordan by her side, Harry stepped over a gray fox den nestled between a deep fold in her back quarter acre where she'd planted Petit Manseng grapes. Foxes love grapes, or any sweet things.

Tucker, his snout smushed down in the opening, announced, *"Vixen! I can smell old chicken bones."*

A fox's voice from within called, *"I killed that chicken fair and square, Bubble Butt."*

Pewter, daintily following the dog and Mrs. Murphy, paw midair, shrieked with delight at the female fox's declaration. *"Bubble Butt! She called you Bubble Butt. See, I'm not the only one that recognizes your more ridiculous qualities."*

"Don't worry, she heard you," Tucker snapped, a little embarrassed.

"I did," said the fox. *"You can hear Fatty Screwloose for acres when she runs her big flannel mouth."*

Appalled at the insult, Pewter flashed to the den's opening, pushing aside the dog. *"How dare you? Come out of there and I'll pull every whisker from your pointy face."*

"*Come in here and say that to my pointy face,*" the gray fox challenged.

Enraged, Pewter stuck her head farther into the den.

Sensible as usual, Mrs. Murphy warned, "*Don't go in there. She has every advantage.*"

"*For one thing, I'm not fat,*" the fox sang out, enjoying herself.

Pewter moved in a bit farther, to stare into two golden eyes. She hit reverse in a hurry, waddling back out comically.

Tucker held her tongue.

Pewter sat for a moment, licking her paw.

"*Come on, Pewts,*" Mrs. Murphy told her. "*Time to keep up.*" Neither she nor Tucker was fooled by the cat's studied nonchalance.

The three animals scampered up to be with Harry and Neil.

The gray fox emerged from her den to watch. Ever curious about humans and domesticated animals, she wondered how on earth they could get along, but they seemed to do just fine. She liked Harry's grapes, so she somewhat liked Harry. Sometimes seeds dropped; some corn kernels from a little patch were tasty. This was a perfect location for a den. Occasionally, Tucker would drop and forget a bone nearby. Those were treasures. But still, spending your life following an animal lurching around on two legs? Seemed odd, and perhaps undignified. Humans were so slow, but the two cats and the dog willingly poked along.

"Right here I have a pH of seven." Harry turned over some dirt with her boot tip. "I'd like to get it to six point five."

"Let me give you Centerpoint," said Neil. "It's one of my best products. Given that you want to experiment with a small portion—what, four by four feet?"

"Right," Harry answered.

"Spread it by hand, or if you have one of those walking spreaders, the type people use for small lawn areas, that will do it. Mark your corners and I promise you next harvest you'll see a difference."

"All right."

"You're fortunate to have good soil. Well, good soil for Virginia. Davis loam. Some alluvial deposits."

"Most of the lower fields are like that, but Dad really kept at them and when I was little we could use muck from the Bay." She meant the Chesapeake Bay. "Can't do that now, but that really helped here. We could also use crushed oyster shells."

"Calcium," Neil said, nodding. "Well, that's the best, but since those things are off-limits now, these commercial applications do provide the same things: calcium, selenium, potassium, magnesium, and on and on the list goes. Soil tests are so accurate today they can pinpoint the exact application you need for your specific crop. Much more cost-effective."

"Until you hit red clay." She scuffed some dirt with the toe of her boot.

"Harry, we can even enrich that these days. Clay has important uses. The reason so many early Virginian homes are brick is thanks to that red clay. It's the devil to dig up. But I mean it, fertilizer today helps even that."

They turned to walk back to Harry's house, about a half mile away, glowing in gorgeous afternoon light.

"Neil, how'd you wind up selling fertilizer and other ag products? You didn't go to ag school."

"My college major was business and I liked it okay, but an old girlfriend, premed, goaded me into organic chemistry. She said it was the washout course for premed and that included vet premed, too. First, I had to take regular chemistry. Liked it. Then I took organic and found I loved it. But what could I do with it? I didn't want to be a medical student."

"I think you are the only person I have ever heard say that they loved organic chemistry." She smiled.

"Actually, a lot of people do, but you have to have a feeling for it, because it's not always logical like, say, mathematics is. Magic happens in those equations." He grinned. "Anyway, I graduated from Amherst with a business degree and starting working at a Monsanto satellite company outside of Minneapolis—great city, by the way. That's when I realized that, much as I did like the business end of the company, I truly liked the hands-on, using the products. Monsanto gets attacked all the time for their genetic engineering of seeds, etc., but I learned a lot, and, Harry, how are we going to feed billions? Twenty-five million babies are born annually in India and seventeen million are born each year in China. They want Western foods, technology, all our goodies."

"What's the number of births annually in the U.S., if you know it?"

"Four point three million."

"Ah." The implications were becoming dreadfully clear. "All those people in developing countries . . . if they can't get enough to eat, seems to me there will be tremendous instability."

"There already is," he said with conviction. "Anyway, I started thinking about what to do to make money based on what I was learning, and I decided to go out on my own selling fertilizer. There are good companies that I can call on, get the best products, and, of course, buy in bulk from Mosaic, PotashCorp. I work with the best. Even companies like Bayer, which made their fortunes in other areas in the late nineteenth century, the early twentieth, now have ag arms. Food is the future, not doctors."

"I believe that."

"Harry, in the next forty years, farmers will need to produce more than they have in the past ten thousand, and the biggest grain producer in the world is still the United States and it will always be. Huge corn producer, too."

"That I know. No other nation in the world has the soils, the variety of climate, that we do. But that huge midwestern belt is gold, pure gold. And we are bound by two huge oceans and have the Gulf right in the middle of the country. Fishing alone is worth billions."

"Like everything else, it's politicized. Do I think we need to carefully manage our resources? I do. It's a tightrope walk, so either some of the environmentalists give a little ground or ultimately millions will starve to death and then a billion or so. There will be nine billion people by 2050 and I think you and I might still be alive then."

"Who knows?" Harry shrugged. "But I can see you do your homework."

"I wouldn't be in business if I didn't."

"*He kind of smells like fertilizer, don't you think?*" Tucker said.

"*It's a medley of smells.*" Mrs. Murphy flared her nostrils.

They reached the back porch.

"Come on in for a Co'Cola or maybe something stiffer," offered Harry.

"Too early for that." He smiled. "But I could use something cold."

"I have some iced tea. Always have it, even in winter."

"Sounds good."

The animals walked into the kitchen, where Pewter took up her post next to her bowl, just in case.

As Neil sipped his beverage, Harry unfolded the soil map with the plan of her farm.

Neil studied it again. "You're very fortunate."

"I am. Given your business and your outlook for the future, I mean that population growth, how do you feel about housing development?"

"In the next ten years Richmond and its surrounding area is supposed to grow by four hundred thousand people. That means good farmland goes under."

"Does. Well, it's happening here."

"Yes, it is, but if developers will plan entire communities with common gardens, wild spaces, stuff like that, or even build more row houses that share an exterior wall, maybe we can limit the damage. People have to live somewhere and not everyone is meant for a high-rise, especially in Virginia. People don't move to Albemarle County to live in a skyscraper. It's much easier to make money as a developer than by farming. We need to find that balance, but profit is what drives all business. There's going to be more development everywhere."

"Wouldn't it make sense for, say, Wesley to buy and build on those acres where the soil is poor?"

Neil leaned back. "Sure. But he also has to consider access to I-64, Route 29, good roads in general. Water. Can wells be dug in places where there is no city water? The whole permitting process is complicated, and like every other county in America, there are people on the board of commissioners dead set against any form of growth or development."

"Right," said Harry. "So why do you and Wesley want Buddy's hundred acres so much?"

"Harry, look where it is! Close to Crozet, a hop to Route 250, maybe a twenty-minute commute to Charlottesville or thirty to Waynesboro, forty minutes to Staunton. Perfect location and the soils seem to be decent, which I don't like to see built upon, but Buddy's got corn smut. Those spores have to be in the soil."

"If he sprays for corn borer, it will somewhat cut down on the smut, not a lot."

"There is no seed treatment for corn smut," Neil said, warming to the subject. "You can remove the galls in a home garden, but not for one hundred acres. So he has to burn or plow under the diseased stalks. Burn, then plow, that's the surest way."

"He can plant a more resistant variety."

"Not for Silver Queen."

"True, but Mexican restaurants like cooking with those galled ears, think it's a delicacy. And they'll pay good money for it."

"Really?" His eyebrows shot up.

"I told Buddy and he called around. Just talked to him this morning, actually. He says he can make more selling to them than he can just selling straight old Silver Queen. It's too late for this crop—it's been on the stalk too long—but he's kind of excited."

"Harry, you never cease to surprise me. Maybe you saved those one hundred acres from development."

"Hey, if I can help out a friend, I will. I don't know if this will help Buddy and his hundred acres, but Tazio and I are going to work to save Random Row. Before Hester was killed, she asked Tazio to head that project. It's the last thing we can do for Hester, and it's the best thing we can do for our special history." She glanced at the calendar on the wall. "Three days until Halloween. Any tickets left?"

"Sold every one." Finishing his drink, he thanked her, then said, "Well, I've got to push off. If you come on out with me, I'll give you the Centerpoint sample now. Have it in the truck. And I'll drop some more by later."

"Great."

Harry happily followed Neil, Tucker in her wake. The dog didn't much like the odor of fertilizer, and said so to the cats.

"Powdery stuff," Mrs. Murphy chimed in. "Goes right up your nose."

"Always smells a little like dead stuff, which I usually like," said the dog, "but you can detect other things, man-made odors."

"Like car exhaust?" Pewter wrinkled her nose and the others laughed.

Ivy Nursery, just west of Charlottesville and the Boar's Head complex, contained long greenhouses as well as trees and other plants in rows outside the buildings.

Harry pulled into the almost full parking lot right before 6 P.M., quitting time for Susan. She walked inside the main building and there to the side was Susan, creating a wonderful boxwood topiary.

"Harry!"

"Said I'd see you on your first day of work. That looks interesting."

"My inspiration is the gardens of Harvey Ladew in Harford County, Maryland. So I'm making this little fox." She put down her shears, pulled off her protective but flexible gloves.

"Let me be your first customer. I'll buy your fox."

"Harry, you don't have to do that."

"I'd love to. He's cute as a button." She touched his boxwood nose.

"My boss saw right away that if I could make foxes and hounds, we'd do a big business. It's taking me some time."

"What do you do, outline it first?"

"That's the thing, you can't really make a good three-dimensional outline. I have all these photographs." She swept her hand in front of six fox photographs leaning against the back of the long table at which she worked. A deep metal sink stood in the corner with glazed pots, terra-cotta pots, and square redwood containers on lined shelves. Ribbons—every color imaginable, including the fashionable gauze ones—lined another shelf, the spools affixed to the edge, a bit of ribbon hanging down from each. The trimming and cutting tools hung above the worktable on a magnetic strip. Filling the workroom were the fragrances of potted plants, small trees, and cut flowers.

"You just eyeballed it?" Harry was incredulous.

"Did."

"You always got A's in art class. Not me."

Susan wiped her hands with a small terry-cloth towel. "You got them in physics."

"I like that he's running," said Harry of the topiary fox.

"I thought it would be easier to do than a sitting fox. But I'll get the hang of it. Hounds, too."

"Susan, you could do dachshunds, Labs, cats. People could give you pictures of their pets."

"Great idea. I'll see if my boss will go for it."

"Who is the boss?"

"Karen Corriss, you remember her? She was three grades ahead of us."

"You mean Karen Dillard?"

"Yeah. She married Rudy Corriss." She lowered her voice. "Apparently he's not doing too well. Real estate."

"I can believe that, but, well"—Harry shrugged—"Ivy Nursery has to be an interesting place to work."

"For one day, it is." Susan laughed. "Okay, let me take pictures of this on my cellphone so I can show Karen my work and my first sale. You're a peach, you know that?"

As Susan took pictures from every angle on her cellphone, Harry beamed. "You never called me a peach before."

"Oh, come on. I have so."

"Sometimes you've called me a good egg. I like peach better."

The two old friends laughed. Susan wrapped a beautiful gauze bow around the fox's neck. "Charlie in gold," she said, calling the fox by his English name. The French use "Reynard."

Harry held up the creation. "Let me get this through the cash register and I'll meet you outside."

They met by Harry's truck, animals in it.

Opening the door, Harry placed the topiary fox on the passenger-seat floor. "Touch that and I pull your whiskers out."

"*Why would I touch it? It's not food.*" Pewter tossed her head.

"Tucker?" Harry stared right into her wonderful corgi's brown eyes.

"*Not me,*" the intrepid dog replied.

"*Don't even ask, I don't chew greenery,*" Mrs. Murphy said.

"*No, you just wrecked last year's Christmas tree,*" Pewter reminded her.

"*I had help.*" The tiger cat's pupils enlarged as she growled at Pewter.

"Enough." Harry shut the door, the window open a crack. "These last two months all those cats have done is fight. And Pewter chases Tucker, too."

"Not for long, I assume," Susan laughed.

"She does need Weight Watchers, doesn't she?"

They stood there in the faltering light, coolness coming on. Shoppers left the nursery, purchases in hand.

Wesley Speer emerged, two huge amaryllises in his arms. Harry, on seeing him, ran up. "Let me help. These are beautiful."

"Thanks, Harry. Hey, Susan. We could have a vestry board meeting right here."

"No quorum," Susan said as she walked with them to Wesley's Lexus SUV.

He opened the back.

"You bought my chest of drawers!" Susan exclaimed.

"Huh?" He stepped back from the inside of the Lexus, a beautiful vehicle and an expensive one.

"My chest of drawers!" repeated Susan. "Baby blue. You went down to Farmville, Number 9, didn't you?"

"I wanted to get something for Rebecca," Wesley said, mentioning his wife. "We often go down there."

"Well, I wanted that one."

"Susan, I bet if you call down there, they'll have another one or can get it for you. This just shows what good taste we both have.

Rebecca dragged me down there, oh, weeks ago and she fell in love with this. I sneaked back today and bought it."

"She'll love you for this." Harry smiled.

He smiled back. "Every now and then it does a husband good to surprise his wife. I thought I'd carry it up to her dressing room, put it by the window, and place the two amaryllises on it."

"Lovely." Susan nodded. "Well, home to Owen. He needs to go outside. I'll see you . . . ?"

"Halloween Hayride, if not before," Wesley answered.

The two women friends returned to Susan's station wagon, parked not far from the old Ford.

Susan kissed Harry on the cheek. "Thank you for making my day."

"You made mine. I have a fox."

Susan put her hand on the door handle. "I can't believe he bought my bureau."

"Honey, Wesley's right. Call them up. It's kind of funny—I'm telling you to spend money and I just spent a little. I didn't even make a fuss."

"Maybe we're exchanging personalities."

"Nah." Harry shook her head. "You can smooth over ruffled feathers, make people feel good. I say what I mean too often and suffer the consequences."

Susan hugged Harry, whom she truly loved. "Harry, I know we are both getting older, because nine times out of ten you now hold your tongue."

"Mmm, five out of ten."

"Six."

"Go on."

"I am," Susan said, slipping behind the wheel.

26

The hum of an overhead fluorescent light distracted Cooper. Outside the police station's windows, the sun was setting. Opening her metal briefcase, she laid out the papers from Hester's folder onto the long table in the conference room.

"Precise," observed Rick, the sheriff, rubbing his chin as he noted a large map with parcels of land and soil types outlined in different colors.

"Sarah was helpful. We went through Hester's papers a few times, and she reiterated that her aunt didn't speak of these much, except to say she was extra vigilant about where and from whom she bought her produce."

He read the numbered key, checked the land to which it referred. "She had properties' sales reports, too, with the price and when land changed hands, which wasn't often."

"From everything we know of Hester, that makes sense. She liked to do business with people she'd done business with for years, preferably whose parents did business with her parents. If a family farm was sold, she wanted to know the new owner's intentions."

"That's one thing about this part of the world. There are times when you can see five generations at a crack."

"Makes you see quite clearly where bad blood galloped from generation to generation." Cooper laughed.

He laughed, too. "Does, but other things, little things—like have you ever noticed that Tally Urquhart, Big Mim, Little Mim, all favor bright blue? Blue signs, blue dresses, blue cars."

"Now that you mention it, they do. Looks like Aunt Tally is going to bust a hundred and one this winter." She paused at the thought of the wise old woman. "I think I'll call on Aunt Tally. She knows these farms, knew them before most of the roads were paved. Maybe there's something we're missing."

The sheriff pushed his chair back from the table. "Coop, any time spent with the old dragon is time well spent, but I don't see the connection between the farms on this map and Hester's death."

She sat staring at the paper, thin where it had been repeatedly folded and unfolded over the years. Pointing to Buddy Janss's holding, she said, "Hester dealt with Buddy for decades. Land value and use are changing. Buddy is certainly aware of it. For one thing, the sale of even one of his parcels would be worth seven figures."

"To Buddy, not to Hester."

"She was opposed to development," said Cooper.

"So is Buddy, up to a point." Tired, Rick's voice betrayed it.

"Chief, I told you about the tie between Josh Hill and Hester. The Virginia tribes connection."

"So they went fishing together," said Rick, his voice now skeptical.

"Here's Morrowdale, where Josh was found," said Cooper, now on a roll. "Hester has a soil outline for it. Also on this map, Hester has all of Neil Jordan's purchases outlined and soil-typed. I keep coming back to this. It has to do with soil, crops, and organic farming, but as far as I know, no one has ever been killed for applying fertilizer."

He smiled. "Not yet anyway."

"But here's where I'm heading. Some of these farms had to have been formerly owned by the Monacans."

He shifted in his seat. "Wouldn't Hester have marked that as well?"

"I don't know. All the stuff Sarah and I found in a folder on land issues, Indian scholarship funds, housing funds, all hinged on proving one's Indian blood to the federal government. I think she might have paid Josh Hill to research who was a Monacan tribe member. We just haven't found his research."

"That's a big jump," he said, holding up his hand. "There is no solid connection between the murders themselves that we know of other than the costumes—no connection to farming practices and no connection to who owned what when."

"Here's where I'm going. The Virginia tribes are not recognized by the federal government, but that doesn't mean they couldn't work to repurchase such lands, nor does it mean they can't continue their pressure on the government as well as the state. The state can't deny them as easily as the feds, but the state would have a difficult time assisting in any purchases."

He threw up his hands. "So what?"

"These lands are worth millions, but they sure wouldn't be if returned or repurchased by a tribe, because they would never come on the market again."

"But if the land was sold now, wouldn't the tribe have to pay fair market value?"

Cooper leaned toward him. "Maybe. Maybe not. There are so many possibilities. Let's say a landowner dies without any heirs. If the state takes over and the tribes create an outcry, they could possibly win the right to reclaim the land or maybe the right to purchase it at a reduced rate."

The lawman remained unconvinced. "But first the tribe has to come up with the money."

"They can open it for fishing and hunting, find new ways to create revenue based on their history and culture, and lastly, even though the Virginia tribes signed away the right to create casinos, they could possibly fight to reclaim those rights. As they are not now recognized by the federal government, think of the fight— a long fight, national attention, with billions at stake! The federal government would look really bad, and what if the timing was just right, say, during a presidential election? A great case could be made that the Monacans' rights were signed away and stolen under duress. This could be huge." She paused. "In Alexandria, preservationists want to save Carver School—built in 1944 for African American children, which means tribal children, too. The purchase price is $675,000. For Alexandria, right outside of D.C., that is not bad. If they succeed, it will energize other preservationists. Obviously, the focus is African American. They may not know about Plecker."

He drummed his fingers on the table. "Billions of dollars, that seems to me to be more motivation for murder than protecting an ancestral school or home."

"To us, but we're white."

This struck the sheriff. "Coop, you're grasping at straws, but one of those straws might be the right one. I'll call the chief of the Upper Mattaponi. I don't fully understand the hopes of the various Virginia tribes."

Cooper refolded the map. "Had another thought. Halloween is Thursday. We might want to assign extra people to the hayride."

"We're stretched thin as it is," he said. "I've assigned extra officers to the downtown mall. It's bound to get rowdy. If a private function gets out of control, we'll be called, but the mall is public. I can't really spare anyone."

"If our killer is as arrogant as I think he is, the hayride could be a perfect venue for more of his showmanship."

"Arrogant, yes, but we still haven't got a compelling motive for these murders, and I don't see how the Halloween Hayride, a fund-raiser for the library, ties to the two killings, other than people will be in scary costumes."

27

*T*he fact that October 29 was forever marked as Black Friday hovered in Harry's consciousness. Not much of a history buff, she was reminded by the media, as were most people, of the dark day when Wall Street went to hell in a handbasket. Of course, panics and depressions had occurred before but, thanks to radio and newsreels, 1929 slid the whole country into debt, disillusionment, and death in front of the entire world. The news media fed the panic.

Just lately, a second depression, called the Great Recession, was broadcast live by cable TV, radio, the Internet, and every possible form of instant communication. Same old, same old, no matter how you sliced and diced it. That was Harry's logic as she pondered life from her tractor seat. She plowed under her harvested barley field. She allowed her sunflowers and the small patch of cornstalks to stand as she thought of how history is a shadow dogging your every step.

Finishing up her work in bright sunshine, the temperature a remarkable sixty-four degrees, she bumped along in the old reliable machine, kicking up dust, driving back to the big shed. Next to her, Tucker had a little seat with a seatbelt. At every lurch, her corgi ears would jangle, then straighten out. Made Harry laugh. Sometimes her animals or the wild animals she watched proved so comical, tears would roll down her cheeks.

"Got to check the vital signs," she said, turning off the engine. After unhooking Tucker's seatbelt, she held the dog in one arm, not easy, and climbed down backward off the vehicle.

"*You are very particular,*" the dog accurately noted.

Harry checked the tractor's oil, the fuel line, and the hydraulic line. The only thing she didn't check was tire pressure. She rarely worried about that, although if a big temperature shift occurred, she'd do it.

"Tucker, waste not, want not," said Harry. "If you keep things tip-top, saves money and saves worry, too."

"*Right, Mom,*" answered the corgi. "*I don't waste bones or greenies.*"

A flutter overhead made both domesticated creatures look up. A brilliantly colored male goldfinch perched on a rafter, showing off his plumage. "*Whatcha doing?*" the little fellow asked.

"*Mom's going over her tractor,*" said Tucker. "*She does this every time she finishes a job. Careful.*"

"*Tell her to put out more seed, will you? The bird feeder's getting low.*" Thinking he saw something to eat, he pecked at the rafter. Nope. He spat it out.

"*I'll try, believe me,*" Tucker promised, "*but she doesn't understand. Hey, how come you're on your own? You goldfinches are so social.*"

"*Too much chatter in the flock. I needed a break. Who needs to know the sordid details of everyone's nest? I like being in the tractor shed. Nice and quiet. No one else is here, although in the summers the swallowtails build nests. Pushy, those birds.*"

"*Don't the cats harass you?*" the dog wondered.

"*The gray cat is too fat to harass anybody,*" he chirped with pleasure. "*Now, the tiger, got to keep my eye out for her. Fortunately, she's usually occupied by something else.*"

"Do you talk regularly to any other birds? Birds that fly around farther away than you do?"

As Harry wiped off her greasy hands on an old red cloth, the happy little fellow hopped down on the tractor seat and looked down at Tucker. "Sure," answered the bird. "Birds do love to gossip."

"Ever run into those crows who ate the scarecrow?" asked Tucker.

The goldfinch hopped down to a back fender to get closer. "I heard you were there with the cats. The crows complained you all spoiled a great find, but they didn't know who killed the human, if that's what you want to know. They said he was fresh meat. So he was killed close by, maybe even killed in a car or something."

"We kind of stumbled upon it. Did you talk to anyone who knew about the murdered witch at the church?"

"No, but I heard about it. When you live in a flock, news travels fast. And I also socialize with birds other than goldfinches," he said proudly, bragging at how cosmopolitan he was. "Anyway, I don't know anything about that witch except people seem to like killing one another, so what's it to you?"

"My human is curious, plus she liked the witch lady. She wants to catch whoever did it."

The bird cocked a snapping black eye at the corgi. "You need better control over her. She's wasting her time. Now, spending more time on her fields, that will yield something of value."

Tucker's attention was diverted by a vehicle coming down the driveway. The sound sent her flying out of the tractor shed to bark warnings.

"Dogs are idiots." The goldfinch laughed as he hopped to the other rear fender, getting closer to Harry.

The slender woman turned around, hands cleaner, beheld the small brilliantly colored bird. "Hello," she said.

"Hello back at you," he chirped, which sounded to her ears like "potato chips."

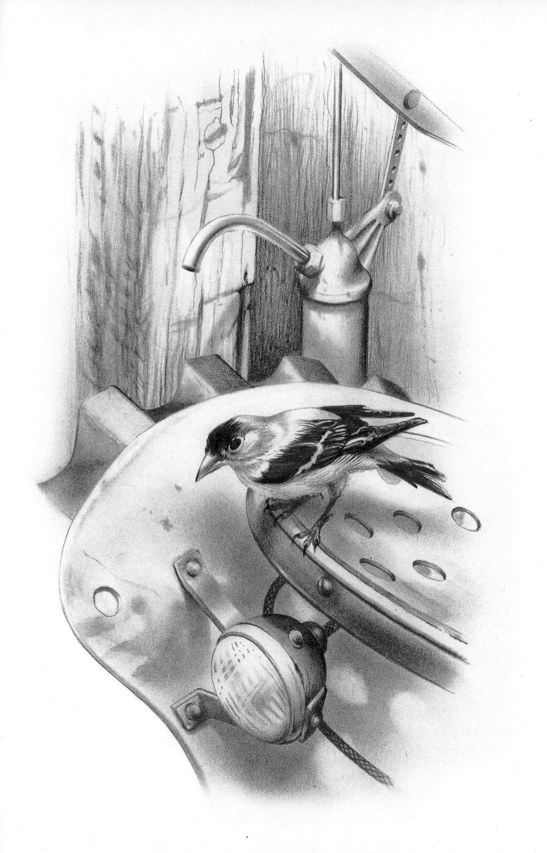

Hearing the familiar goldfinch call, she smiled. "You're a bold fellow."

She hung up the red rags, walked out of the shed, glanced over her shoulder. The goldfinch chirped, then flew up to the rafter.

"Hey," Cooper called out, Tucker at her heels.

"Is this a courtesy call or business? I never know when you're in uniform," Harry said.

"I was down at Rose Hill. Thought I'd stop by on my way back to town."

The two fell in side by side as they made their way to the house.

"How's Aunt Tally?" Harry asked. Rose Hill was the old lady's estate.

"Never changes. She's besotted with the baby."

The two walked into the sunny kitchen.

"Is she dispensing advice?" Harry asked, raising an eyebrow.

"No, she's leaving that up to Big Mim, who, by all accounts, is a treasure trove of childrearing wisdom."

They laughed.

Before they sat, Harry asked, "Coffee, tea, Co'Cola, hot chocolate?"

"Nothing, thanks." Cooper took a seat at the table. "Harry, I asked Aunt Tally a lot of questions about Hester, about ownership of old farms, stuff like that. Someone should record what she remembers before it goes with her." Cooper felt that every old person was a library.

"Good idea," said Harry, sitting across from her. "Learn anything new?"

The tall deputy nodded. "More than I imagined. Who married whom. How many children, legitimate and non. Who hated whom and who was smart and not. She said such things run in families. I showed her a county map with farms outlined. She knew the history of every single one, and her memory started with the end of World War One. Got really clear in the twenties, but she said with her parents, her friends' parents, and their grandparents—well, the living memories recounted to her when she was young, all put together, reached back to the 1830s. She could just rattle stuff off.

"She pointed out which farms had been well managed, even through the Depression, World War Two, and up to today. She knew where some of the old slave graveyards were, and even where there are Indian mounds, which may or may not be graveyards. Most of that history has been lost. She said if you have an ancestor in a graveyard, you have a legal right to tend to that graveyard once a year. She noted farms that had endured ups and downs, and much of that seemed to tie in to drinking. Then there were those who lost everything." Cooper sighed. "I hit a dead end. Learned a lot, but . . ."

"Any disputes?" asked Harry. Aunt Tally could always tell a good story.

"Not as many as you would think. A lot of squabbling among heirs in certain families. Any dispute she recounted seemed to involve wine, women, moonshine." Cooper laughed.

"Never a bad place to start."

Cooper, hat off, ran her fingers through her ash-blonde hair. "I'm pretty frustrated."

"I can understand that," said Harry. "Look, I know I get in the way, but let me make a suggestion. Hester, though well educated, was country. I'm a Smith graduate but country. I can help."

Cooper shook her head at her neighbor and friend. "You? Harry, one of these days you'll either fall into a well or get yourself killed."

"Now, just a minute here. Hear me out. Let's go to Hester's house. Let me go through her truck, the outbuildings where she kept equipment. If we don't find anything of interest, then let's go to her roadside stand."

"You don't want to go into the house?" Cooper's curiosity rose. Despite herself, she wanted to understand Harry's logic.

"No. Like I said, I'm country, Hester was country. I can look at equipment, tools, trucks, tractors, and see things you don't."

"Like what?"

"Let's find out," Harry egged her on.

Challenged face-to-face, Cooper had to say yes.

Cooper called ahead and asked permission from Sarah to comb the outside grounds and equipment. Sarah readily agreed.

In the barn, pulling open every drawer of Hester's freestanding toolbox, Harry found old tools but nothing that proved helpful. She ran her hands along the inside walls of the shed—no false boards or hiding places. She opened the small box behind the tractor seat, finding the manual. She lifted up the seat. Carefully searching each outbuilding, examining each piece of equipment, she even looked into the bins holding birdseed, sticking a broom handle down into them and twirling it around.

Cooper admired Harry's thoroughness. "Hiding something in a seed bin—now, that's clever, though there's nothing here."

"Moonshine is often hidden that way, just like when it's trucked, it's generally hidden in the middle of another shipment, like furniture boxes. Or before flyovers with infrared cameras,

when the boys would grow marijuana, it would usually be in the middle of a corn crop. That doesn't work anymore." Harry looked around the shed. "Let me check her truck. She spent a lot of time in it; she told me it was on its third set of tires."

Before going into the cab, Harry pulled off the hubcaps. "Cooper, pull the ones on the other side. Hubcaps can be good storage if you're careful."

Using her penknife, Cooper popped off the hubcaps, took a look, then replaced them. Next she opened the truck's passenger-side door as Harry opened the one on the driver's side.

"Our team went over the truck," said Cooper.

"I know," said Harry, though she continued searching, unde-terred.

In the glove box, they found the usual: manual, registration, insurance information, old pens, a box of Altoids. From the side pocket, Harry fished out one earring, a notebook, which she leafed through, a powerful LED flashlight, and bits of leaf, dirt. Leaning over the steering wheel, she ran her palm over the dash.

"Damn," Harry cursed low.

"I told you we went over it."

"Pull up the floor mat." Harry did it on her side of the truck and tossed the rubber mat outside. "There's the covering that came with the vehicle underneath. Take your penknife and slowly work around that to see if anything lifts up." As Harry did this on the driver's side, excitement crept into her voice. "I think I've got something."

She raised the loose edge of the original mat and carefully slid her hand underneath it. "Aha—here's something . . . ," she said, and pulled out a flat manila envelope with a clasp. "Let's see what we've got." She hurried to the back of the truck and dropped the tailgate.

Now next to her, Cooper watched as Harry drew papers and a

map from the envelope and gently spread the map on the truck bed.

"Same as the other map . . ." Cooper's voice trailed off.

Harry squinted. "Some properties have parcels that are outlined in purple."

Cooper grabbed some papers. "Here's the key. The purple signifies ancestral land." She pointed to a spot on a nearby farm. "Here's a Quaker school near Midway Farm. That school's gone now. Boy, is this thorough!"

Cooper flipped through the other pages. "This is Josh Hill's research," she said, pointing to his name on a document. "Look here. Says the Virginia tribes cared greatly about education."

Harry exclaimed, "Some of this goes back to right after the Revolutionary War. He has a note here, 'Many of us took Quaker names. The Quakers have been consistently helpful identifying and helping the Monacans and other tribes to reclaim our lands.'"

She picked up an old newspaper clipping. "Here's an article about how the Upper Mattaponi purchased land and restored Sharon Indian School, which is the only Indian school on the Virginia Landmarks Register and the National Register." Harry checked the map again. "Hill drew double lines around old church schools, Random Row, and also where old churches used to stand. And hey, about forty acres of Buddy's one hundred acres are marked off in purple."

Cooper leaned over and studied this after setting down a paper she'd just been examining. "Hill wrote out a plan for raising money to purchase Random Row and part of Buddy's land, saying it would be easier to prove tribal usage there, even with Walter Ashby Plecker's paper genocide."

Harry straightened up at the ramifications of Hill's report.

Cooper continued. "He wrote that while church lands were

carefully recorded, the buildings had usually disappeared after a century and more, but, and he underlined 'but' in red, with the School Desegregation Act of 1965, the records for schools are much more recent." She put her forefinger to her lips. "The problem goes back to how to prove you're a Virginia Indian."

"If someone like Josh or Hester could arouse interest among the African American community to jointly preserve history—say, at Random Row—working together would render that less important," said Harry. "Here's a list of local people Hill thought might help their efforts."

"Your name is on there," Cooper remarked.

Harry stared at her name, along with the names of professors, businesspeople, and community leaders, white, black, and tribal. "Tazio's name is on here, too. Hill did his homework."

"And he paid for it," said Cooper.

"Hester did, too. She must've hid these documents because she was afraid. She didn't want this information to fall into the wrong hands and all of this research to be destroyed."

Cooper whistled. "Those that would gain by this being destroyed are Buddy, Wesley, and maybe Neil, as they often work together on land purchases."

"They don't seem like murderers," said Harry, mulling it over. "Wesley and Neil are on the vestry board. Buddy is the sweetest man ever."

"People can fool you." Cooper thought a long time. "I can't arrest three men on suspicion of murder with only a map and these papers to go on. And there is the good possibility they have nothing to do with it. But I'm nervous about what might happen at the hayride, and it's only two days away."

"Can you assign extra security to it?"

"I can try again." Cooper called her boss and pleaded her case once more.

Finally Rick relented and said he'd assign Dabny to work with her.

"Thanks, boss." Cooper clicked off her cellphone. "Dabny."

"One more is better than none." Harry folded her arms across her chest. "Thursday night is going to be interesting."

"I hope not," Cooper said, though she feared the worst. Halloween had never seemed so frightening.

28

*H*alloween colors, orange and black, gave way to shimmering slate on Thursday night as twilight fell over the rolling Virginia countryside. Those trees without leaves appeared outlined in charcoal, and the conifers swayed blue and silver. The pin oaks, dried leaves still attached, rustled in the light breeze. When the wind lifted their leaves upward, the pale underside contrasted with the tree's dark bark. Then as the wind died down, they turned right side up.

As the sun set, the actors for the Halloween Hayride met at Random Row's middle schoolhouse, along with the starter, Lolly Currie; Neil, who would keep reports on traffic midway through the hayride; and two boys charged with keeping the goblins lit. The number of people totaled thirteen, the ideal number for a Halloween drama. While they reviewed their parts, a molten sky faded to blue velvet.

"Darkening of the moon," said Wesley. "What luck. We can scare the pants off everyone." He laughed as he glanced out the long windows.

"You do that anyway, Wes," Neil remarked.

Tazio focused on the task at hand, once more reviewing the night's plans. At her side was Lolly, with a duplicate schedule on her clipboard. "Okay," said Tazio. "First hay wagon leaves from the barn at seven P.M. After that, the wagons leave at ten-minute intervals and we have . . ."

"Ten wagons plus foot followers," Paul reminded her, and Tazio was grateful for the strong man's presence at her side.

"Why are people going on foot?" Wesley wondered.

"Some people like to walk and some groups won't all fit in the wagons. We'll put the children in first and have the adults walk alongside the wagons," Tazio replied.

"How many people can we expect tonight?" Cooper had just finished putting on her Jeepers Creepers costume.

"Three hundred and twenty-one," Tazio said. "That's how many bought tickets. That doesn't mean all will come out. The library also received contributions from over one hundred people who won't be here. After expenses, we net over twenty thousand dollars. Pretty good. Paul, we can't thank you enough for getting the horse-drawn wagons and drivers to contribute their services, and Reverend Jones, you organized the truck-drawn wagons. We have four of those. They'll be good backups if a problem arises with the horses."

"I trust the horses more than engines," Reverend Jones replied.

"Okay. First scare, after Lolly gives the initial go-ahead. The wagon rolls by the schoolhouse, Dr. Frankenstein has the monster on the table." She glanced over at Buddy Janss, a credible if rotund Frankenstein's Monster. "Buddy breaks the bands, rises up, chokes Dr. F after a suitable struggle, then flees the building, running into the cornfield, threatening folks on the wagon. Then he runs back into the corn and sneaks into the schoolhouse, gets on the table, and does it all over again."

Lolly read from her schedule, "After that, 'glowing goblins and ghosts flutter through the cornfield as the wagon progresses.' How you guys made those things work, I'll never know."

"Pretty much the same way you make a jack-o'-lantern." Paul smiled at the two high school boys who had created the goblins and ghosts. "They're lit by LEDs, and they go up and down, back and forth on wires, using the tiny battery packs in their backs."

Brows wrinkling for a moment, Tazio asked Neil, "No one using candles tonight, or torches?"

"No, too dangerous," said Neil. "We have a fake torch at the end, when the monk"—he nodded to Reverend Jones—"calls the spirits to order and points the wagons toward the old Mount Carmel Church, where it all ends festively."

"And safely," the reverend reminded them.

"All right," said Tazio. "After the goblins and ghosts, Frankenstein's Monster should be back in the schoolhouse, ready for the next wagon. Okay. Now, the first wagon goes between the two big trees on either side of the dirt lane."

"That's my cue." Cooper smiled in her Jeeper Creepers costume. "And given that I need to get hooked up to a darned cable, I'm leaving now." What she didn't say was that Dabny, who would fasten her to the guy wire between the trees, would be observing from an old farmside road along the edge of the cornfield, ready in case trouble occurred.

From her perch in either of the trees she would swing between, Cooper would have as good a view as possible, given it was five days after the dark of the moon. Both on-duty officers would have cellphones, but should a cellphone not properly work, Cooper and Dabny also carried a piercing whistle.

"Once people recover from the Jeepers Creepers scare," said Tazio, "they round the bend and the Headless Horseman gallops toward them before going into the open-air shed, disappearing from the hay wagon's sight. Is there any way to throw a pumpkin for a head from there?" Tazio asked her boyfriend.

"It would scare the driving horses," said Paul. Despite his assigned role, his head was always screwed on straight. "Basically, I'll be running toward them, then veering off. We did set out a jack-o'-lantern on a fence post about a quarter of a mile down the road from me and Dinny." He named his horse, a lovely old hunting fellow who had done it all, seen it all.

"Neil, you're all in black near the shed," said Tazio. "If the wagons need to move along, you call Lolly. Hopefully, no one will see you as our secret traffic manager."

"Right." Neil nodded to Tazio.

"The wagons pass the hayfield, large rolls stacked together. There will be a green-eyed goblin on top—again courtesy of our high-tech guys. Then, the evil Jason and his chainsaw, meaning you, Blair"—she tipped her paper toward Little Mim's husband— "will jump out from behind the tall obelisk in the graveyard."

"And I'll turn on the ghost noises and wails from the graveyard before I jump out," Blair added with enthusiasm.

"We've got lights on one bony arm coming up from a fake grave—we didn't want to desecrate a real one," said Tazio. "We were going to have a witch in the graveyard, but after Hester's death that seemed insensitive."

"Good thinking," Neil complimented her. "Jason beheads the vampire, Count Dracula, who is the undead, so of course he just puts his head back on."

"You've always had a good head on your shoulders." Reverend Jones laughed at Barry Betz, the batting coach whom Cooper had started dating. Barry would portray Dracula this evening.

As Cooper had talked him into it, everyone assumed the relationship between them was heating up. They were right.

"Any questions?" asked Tazio.

"We aren't allowed to drink inside the meeting room at Mount Carmel, right?" Wesley asked.

"Now, Wesley, when has anyone been allowed to drink inside a church building?" Reverend Jones winked at him.

"Right." Wesley smiled.

"The second hay wagon, the one pulled by the team of Belgians, has a full bar under the driver's seat, since we knew how parched some of you can get from your labors." Tazio smiled broadly.

"Belgians . . . ?" Neil looked for direction.

"The cream-colored draft horses," Paul informed him.

"Ah." Neil nodded. "I'm glad to know the Belgian is a horse of a different color."

"We've got this covered," said Tazio. "It's going to be the most exciting Halloween Hayride this county has ever seen." She laughed. "And I'm the Fallen Angel who appears as the hay wagon reaches Mount Carmel, holding up a crucifix to our vampire, head back on, who shrinks and screams in horror, vanquished at last. Hey, we've thought of everything."

"What about the kids who wet their pants?" Wesley joked.

"That's up to Mom and Dad. By now they should know to bring Handi Wipes and towels."

Waiting back in the last wagon, which was being pulled by the Haristeens' truck, Pewter complained as she shifted to find a comfortable spot on the hay bale. *"By the time we get to the church, there won't be any food left. We're the caboose."*

"Sure there will be," said Tucker, an expert on dropped treats. She confidently predicted, *"Stuff falls on the floor."*

"Tucker, here's a frightening Halloween idea: I'll jump on the table and make everyone scream, 'Get the cat off the table!' Now, that's really scary."

Mrs. Murphy laughed. *"Pewter, you jump on that table and Mom will smack you. Then you'll be the one screaming and that will scare the children."*

"I'm going inside the truck," said Pewter, who leapt from the wagon's hay bale to the truck bed, also full of hay. She started smacking the sliding window. *"Release me from these trolls!"*

Harry moved forward in the fluffed hay to also knock on the window. In the driver's seat, Fair turned around and slid it open.

"Honey, Pewter's being a pill. Will you take her with you?" Then she said to Susan's husband, Ned, sitting in the passenger seat, "Ned, she'll be on your lap."

"Fine with me as long as she doesn't drive."

Harry grunted as she picked up the fat cat, passing her through the open back window.

Fair asked, "Do you have the .38?"

"I do."

Ned looked at Fair with alarm. "What's going on?"

Harry nonchalantly replied, "Better to have it and not need it than need it and not have it."

Susan, sitting next to Miss Mona in the wagon bed, patted the old lady's hand. Miss Mona's walker was strapped to the back tailgate. A stroke had affected her mobility, which sometimes embarrassed her, but the group of old friends pretended she was the Miss Mona they knew in childhood. She was, except that she couldn't get around like she used to.

BoomBoom tended to Colonel Friend, also very old. Colonel Friend was a bemedaled World War II vet. Bunny Biedecke, another World War II vet, leaned against a small hay bale as he sat in the sweet-smelling fluffed hay. Dear old Bunny was already asleep. BoomBoom's partner, Alicia, sat next to him. Bunny had to have been tired, because he was the kind of fellow who would normally revel in the experience of sitting next to a beautiful woman. Come to think of it, most of the men in Crozet fit into that category.

Tazio had interspersed the trucks with the horse-drawn wagons. If a horse threw a shoe, the people could get back to a truck wagon; these held fewer people but there was also room in the truck's bed. Most people wanted to ride in the horse-drawn wagons, but some enjoyed the truck-drawn ride, mostly because all the kids were clustered together, noisy with excitement, in the horse-drawn wagons.

Aunt Tally hotly refused getting stuck with "old people," as she called them. She sat in the first horse-drawn wagon up with the driver, regaling him, so she thought, with stories of her youth and her own "excellent" driving abilities. Big Mim grimly sat behind, fearing Aunt Tally had hidden a small flask in her heavy cardigan sweater.

As the mercury dropped, the screams rose up. Waiting to move forward, Harry and the passengers in the last wagon could hear them as they pierced the night in sequence. The temperature fell into the mid-forties. The beautiful stillness of this velvet black Halloween meant they could even hear the bellows of fright from the graveyard, a good mile and a half distant.

Checking his texts, Ned noted when the seventh wagon had been challenged by the Headless Horseman. "Okay, Fair, roll," he ordered. "Lolly says we're up. Neil said wagon number seven just passed him."

Watch in hand, Lolly was standing just outside the first school-house. She had wanted to do something to honor her boss's memory, so she had volunteered for the job of starter in Hester's pet project. Lolly was good with details. Dressed in a skeleton costume, the young woman checked and rechecked her watch and various texts. Naturally, some wagons clattered along more slowly than others, but in the main, the evening's planned event was running quite smoothly. All seriousness, Lolly would call out each passing wagon's number and say, "Move out."

In the last wagon, driving at fifteen miles an hour, the cats, dogs, and humans passed the middle schoolhouse. Eerie lights showed a large beaker bubbling froth in green light. Dr. Franken-stein's Monster lifted his bulky head. The doctor poised over him, gigantic hypodermic needle in hand. *Snap*, the bonds broke, falling away as the monster reached up with his right hand, grabbing Dr. Frankenstein by the throat. The furious struggle was enhanced by the green light. The contents of the giant needle shot upward in the air as the doctor helplessly sank to his knees. The monster threw up his hands in triumph, not unlike a football player in the end zone. He whipped his head around as best he could, despite the spike in his neck, then crashed out the side door, roaring as he did, rushing at the wagon. Hearing the riders' screams, he then turned to disappear into the cornfield. As the wagon moved forward, one could hear the cornstalks bending and rustling.

"Good scream," Susan complimented Harry.

Pewter, on Fair's lap, pupils wide, meowed, "*I don't like the monster's face.*"

The back window, left open so Harry and Susan could holler at their husbands, allowed Mrs. Murphy and Tucker to hear Pewter. It sounded like a tiny meow to the two men in the cab.

"*Scaredy-cat,*" the two animals teased.

"*Piffle,*" the gray cat replied. "*I just don't like Frankenstein's face. I'm not scared.*"

The truck crept forward and for a moment they heard the far-off clip-clop of the draft horses pulling the cart in front of them, so still was the night.

"Don't you love the sound of hoofbeats?" Shawl wrapped around her shoulders, Miss Mona smiled.

"I do." Harry held one hand while Susan held the other. "Miss Mona, your hand is cold. Let's put on your gloves."

As they did that, two glowing goblins and two ghosts fluttered above the cornfield, moving from side to side, then up, only to sink back down.

Ahead, they heard an explosive scream of fright.

"Must be really scary," Miss Mona said to Colonel Friend.

"We'll see." His voice quavered, but as he'd fought his way through Europe, it's doubtful too much could rattle the colonel.

As they were poised between the two trees, branches twisting into the night, out flew Jeepers Creepers. So sudden and silent was this attacking nasty bird/human, wings outstretched, strange face looking down with a snarl, that even Harry drew deeper into the hay.

"Kill! That bird wants to kill us!" Pewter screamed.

Even Tucker barked in surprise, then breathed out in relief. "It's Coop!" The corgi had recognized Cooper's scent.

Mrs. Murphy inhaled the crisp air. "So it is. She scared me."

High in the tree, Cooper folded her wings and gazed over the scene. She could see a little bit around the curve, back to the schoolhouses, which stood like clapboard rectangles in the darkness. Buddy was running through the cornfield, charged by Count Dracula. This seemed to be an impromptu scare as the last wagon rolled by. Now that Harry, Fair, and the others had passed, Cooper prepared to push off hard on the zipline and swoop in the opposite direction to get back into the tree and climb down.

As Fair slowly took his passengers around the big curve, out charged the Headless Horseman with a menacing howl, cape flying behind him, hoofbeats clattering.

Through the fake neck, Paul could see pretty well. His horse, Dinny, wondered why they just kept going into the shed again and again. His job was to chase hounds who were chasing foxes. This back-and-forth stuff was boring, but being a good soul, he did as he was asked, ears twitching as people screamed. What a racket!

Next to Fair in the cab, Ned remarked, "That horse could be in a movie."

Fair, Dinny's physician, chuckled. "Dinny is dipped in gold."

Sighing, Ned absentmindedly stroked Pewter's head as she chose to grace his lap with her large presence. "I've been a horse husband for twenty-three years," said Ned. "I'll bet I've spent more money on horses, tack, and membership fees to hunt clubs than I did on my children's college educations."

"No doubt, but you have a happy wife," said Fair. "Think of the men who don't."

Ned laughed. "Point well taken."

Miss Mona, ears still keen, said to Susan, "I hear screams behind us."

Susan nodded. "Over in the hayfield."

The jack-o'-lantern flickered ominously, on the fence post at the end of the hayfield.

Buddy Janss, still dressed as Frankenstein's Monster, clambered up one of the hay rolls, kicking the man dressed as Dracula as he tried to follow. Finally, the faux vampire grasped his ankle, pulling down the huge fellow. From a distance, Dracula appeared to bite the monster in the neck as Frankenstein bellowed, then fell still. Dracula opened his cape, slipping his knife into his belt. He also carried a small pistol but didn't use it on Frankenstein. The noise would have proven too distracting. As it was, those viewing the drama thought Frankenstein had been bitten, which he was. He was stabbed, too.

Bloodcurdling screams filled the air, the perfect cover for real mayhem. This Halloween Hayride was topping all prior ones for thrills.

The big square churchyard, hand-laid stone fence surrounding it, hove into view. The obelisk shone silver. As they approached, Harry could read the name on the monument: VILLION.

From behind the obelisk, movie villain Jason appeared, chain saw in hand, white mask in place. Swinging the saw around like a hammer throw, he advanced toward them. The chain saw was not turned on, but that didn't lessen the startling effect. As he rushed them, wailing ghost noises from the graveyard added to the drama.

From the hayfield, Count Dracula ran hard, jumping the low stone wall at the other end of the graveyard, fangs dripping blood as he headed toward Jason.

"Oh, look at the bony arm reaching out from the grave." Miss Mona shivered a moment.

The colonel nodded, for he had seen this sort of thing in real life. He'd seen much, maybe too much.

Despite the screams, Bunny Biedecke remained asleep.

Jason turned to meet his attacker and swept the chain saw at Dracula, whose head tumbled off backward. But being undead, the Count picked it up, put it right back on. The two creatures struggled; the Count grappled with Jason, biting him in the neck. Jason fell to the ground, grabbing his neck, fake blood shooting through his fingers.

Using one hand, Dracula vaulted over the graveyard stone wall to disappear. As the wagon slowly passed, Jason rose up, returning to the graveyard.

Hearing a strangled cry, Little Mim's husband, Blair, pulled off his Jason mask and walked to peer over the other side of the graveyard wall. On his side, trying to clear his throat and his head, was Barry Betz, the original Dracula.

"Barry! Barry!" Blair said, hopping over.

The young man couldn't yet speak. Blair looked over the field and beheld another person dressed as Count Dracula running toward Tazio, as had been planned.

"Watch out!" Blair shouted to Tazio.

She turned, holding up her cross as the Fallen Angel, but this final time Dracula did not shrink back as scripted. Instead, he struck her hard enough to knock her sideways. Grabbing her, he pulled her up; she struggled to escape until he put a gun to her temple. He dragged her to a dip in the land where he had hidden a dirt bike.

"Get on the bike," he ordered.

Tazio did as she was told. He sat behind her, gun still to her temple. He started the dirt bike. Given that the gas was on the right handlebar, he had to slip the gun into his belt alongside the knife. As the bike picked up speed, Tazio sat still.

From her perch, Cooper could only dimly see the unplanned drama. She didn't have time to punch in numbers on her cellphone, and pulled out the whistle instead.

The piercing note carried across the fields, over the assembled wagons. Dabny fired up the truck, roaring out of the side farm road. He screeched to a halt beneath a tree.

"Get me outta here!" said Cooper. "Something's wrong."

Dabny backed the truck under the tree and stepped up into the bed. He lifted himself from the bed onto the cab and reached a limb. Swinging himself up, he climbed toward Cooper, who was on her way down.

"It's these damned wings."

Dabny unfastened her wings as she tore off the mask. Then they both backed down the tree and got into the truck.

"Graveyard," was all she said.

Within minutes they reached the graveyard, where Blair was helping out an injured Barry.

From the Haristeens' truck bed, Harry shouted to Cooper,

"Some maniac's got Taz!" Harry hopped off the truck and started running after the dirt bike, now churning away from the grave-yard. Mrs. Murphy and Tucker leapt off to follow. In the cab, Pew-ter thought they were crazy. She stayed put, hoping Ned wouldn't join in the ridiculous tumult.

Dabny turned the truck around and headed in the direction in which they last saw the fleeing vampire, with Cooper sitting next to him, straining to see anything.

Riding Dinny back to the schoolhouse, Paul caught a glimpse of Dracula on his bike, carrying the Fallen Angel. The abductor dipped down the other side of a swale in the hayfield.

Leaning forward on the solid horse, Paul galloped toward the spot. When he reached the cusp of the swale, he saw below him what he assumed to be a crazed idiot stop to position Tazio so he could hold her tighter. Without a second of hesitation Paul charged down the low rise and came alongside the dirt bike, which hadn't picked up speed with its cargo. Leaning over, he tried to climb on, and grabbed Dracula's shoulder; Dracula reached for his gun. Paul slid off Dinny like a calf roper and the horse stopped cold.

Paul wrestled the fake vampire to the ground, the bike's wheels spinning as they went over. The young man shoved Dracula away, then grabbed Tazio. Dracula retrieved his gun and remounted his bike. He buzzed off.

Tazio's eyes fluttered as Paul lifted her into his arms.

"It's all right, honey. You're safe." Paul hoisted her onto Dinny's saddle and Tazio slumped forward on the animal's neck. Holding the reins, Paul walked them up the rise, across the northern end of the hayfield. Ahead, he saw Buddy Janss as Frankenstein's Mon-ster, sprawled on a hay bale.

Flagging down Cooper and Dabny, Paul asked for help for Buddy.

"I'll call an ambulance," said Dabny. "Which way did Dracula go?" he asked Paul, who pointed west.

Dabny drove alongside the field in the direction Paul pointed.

Now in the hayfield, Harry ran toward the fiend dressed as Dracula, who pushed the dirt bike for more speed. Evidently, he was still a bit wobbly from Paul's blow.

After loading Barry into the truck, Fair ran, keeping pace about two hundred yards behind Harry, but she was lighter and faster.

After looking over his shoulder to see Harry in pursuit, the attacker circled in the hayfield. He steered his bike behind the hay bales, cutting his engine.

Harry flew through the hay stubble faster than she'd ever run when she was on her college track team.

The dirt-bike Dracula saw that Harry was high up and behind him, but he couldn't see Fair even farther behind. Slowly, he pushed his bike around the hay bales, darkness shielding him.

The darkness also shielded Taz on Dinny's back, but as the attacker pushed his bike he now saw them.

The vampire pulled out a gun and leveled it.

Harry boomed out, "Paul, move!"

Tazio's abductor stopped for a moment as Harry barely touched the earth, heading straight at him, Tucker and Mrs. Murphy in front of her.

Firing, he missed Tazio, then turned and restarted the bike. Switching his gun to his left hand, he revved the engine. He roared straight for Harry, cape flying, mask in place, fangs showing.

As the bike hurtled at her, he fired his revolver with his left hand, wide of the mark. Harry hit the ground and rolled. Cunning, she pulled out the .38. She figured he would be ineffective firing the gun with his left hand.

RITA MAE BROWN & SNEAKY PIE BROWN

Then Dracula spotted Fair running at him, but he slowed and made a one-eighty, again barreling straight for Harry, now back on her feet.

She kept her eyes on his right hand. He had to take his hand off the throttle and switch the gun to his right hand to accurately fire the weapon. That gave her a ray of hope. Bending down, she picked up a handful of dirt and hay stubble with her left hand.

Nearly upon her, he slowed and pulled out his gun.

Harry fired one shot from the .38 at his torso and sent another bullet for the front wheel, too. The tire blew; the bike lurched, then toppled over.

As the rider screamed, Mrs. Murphy leapt onto his arm. Harry threw dirt in the eyeholes of his mask. With her front claws, the cat ripped the mask. He coughed, trying to hold on to the gun. With everything she had, Harry threw herself onto him, smashing the butt of the .38 into his masked head.

In her jaws, Tucker grabbed the man's neck. Blood was running inside his mask where the animals had torn through. Bright crimson blood now poured from the deep fang marks the corgi made, and more blood oozed from Harry's bullet, which had hit a lung. The dog continued biting as Mrs. Murphy nipped and nipped, her sharp claws lethal on small prey and painful on large.

Fair caught up with them. Hauling the man to his feet as he started to come to, Fair hit him so hard Harry heard the man's jaw break.

Having followed the bike's high revs, Cooper and Dabny now arrived, driving across the hayfield, dirt churning behind the truck.

Cooper pulled out her service revolver as Dabny took the snubnose .38 from Harry.

"Tucker, Mrs. Murphy, enough!" Harry commanded.

The cat sank her claws into the mask and pulled at it before it snapped back.

Cooper leaned down and yanked it off.

Harry couldn't believe it. "Neil Jordan!"

His jaw hung, the break obvious, teeth missing.

"You could have been killed!" Fair exclaimed to his wife. "Why would you do something like that?"

"He was going to kill Taz," she said to her husband, Cooper, and Dabny. "And I had Dad's .38. You told me to use it if necessary. I always do what you tell me."

30

"Four people taken away to the hospital," said Harry. "What a Halloween." She, Fair, and Cooper were sitting at the kitchen table.

"Buddy, Taz, Barry, and Neil—and Neil under guard," growled Tucker, sitting on the floor nearby. "If I could have had just a little more time, I could have killed him," bragged the corgi. Perhaps it was true.

Mrs. Murphy sat on Harry's lap. "He's blind in one eye."

"If I'd been with you, I'd have gotten the other one," said Pewter, in Fair's lap.

Tucker laughed at her. "Chicken, you stayed in the truck."

"I jumped in the bed because Miss Mona had a spell while tending to Barry," Pewter explained, or tried to. "She used to be a nurse, you know, back in the 1950s, but it was too much for her." The gray paused. "I had to help."

While this was wishful thinking, neither Mrs. Murphy nor Tucker teased her, because Cooper was now telling the assembled humans just what had happened after the ambulances left.

"We walked into Mount Carmel, told everyone gathered there in the church to stay still, and we counted heads. Wesley Speer was missing. So we drove to the schoolhouse. No Wesley. Put out an alert and picked him up the next morning, boarding a 6:10 A.M. flight to Phoenix out of Dulles. Wesley admits to being an accessory for the first two killings. Said he opposed killing Tazio and Harry. When he heard the shots, he knew Neil was out there. He got scared and ran. He swears he tried to talk Neil out of it on their cellphones. Swears Neil threatened him. Said he turned into a maniac after killing Josh and Hester. Mind you, I take this with a grain of salt. He wants to save his own skin." Cooper paused. "I told Rick we should give Dinny, Mrs. Murphy, and Tucker an award for service to the public."

"*Hey, hey, I helped Miss Mona.*" Pewter put her paws on the table, which Fair removed, settling her back in his lap. "*I did my part,*" she insisted, vainly and in vain.

It was Monday morning, and Cooper had stopped by the farm before going to work.

"How's Buddy?" asked Harry. "I don't want to call Georgia. She's got to be on overload." Georgia was Buddy's wife.

"He'll be okay. Neil stabbed him in the back and must've thought he'd killed him, but Buddy is big, has a lot of muscle as well as fat, and the knife didn't puncture anything vital. That deep wound will take time to heal, but he'll be fine. He goes home today. He had no idea what any of this was about."

"Did Neil confess?" Fair asked.

"Not so far, but his jaw is wired shut. He's blind in one eye. One lung has collapsed. He'll live. Can't talk. We'll get him to write answers to our questions once he's not so drugged up. If he cooperates, that is. I expect he'll lie like a rug." Cooper smiled. "Mrs. Murphy and Tucker did as much damage as you did, Harry. I have never seen anyone run as fast as you once I caught sight of you in the hayfield. Go, girl!"

"Luckily I had my .38. It's amazing what you can do when you have to."

"Brave. And foolish. He had a gun, too." Cooper admired Harry, even though her neighbor had once again taken a wild risk.

Harry shrugged. "So did Wesley say anything else?"

"He did," said Cooper. "Wesley said they stood to realize be-tween twenty to twenty-four million dollars if they could have developed that property behind Random Row. They thought they could get the schoolhouses and develop them, too."

"But Buddy hadn't agreed to sell," Fair said. "Or had he?"

"He was weighing the options," Cooper said. "They kept throwing money at Buddy and figured he'd cave at two and a half million. They'd pay the taxes. That's a big chunk of change."

"Sure is." Harry's eyes widened. "But why kill Hester and Josh? They hadn't yet raised money or gathered people who might raise opposition." Harry knew she would always miss Hester.

"One, they certainly would have done so. With Tazio on board, they would have been a formidable team. Hard to deny the worth of their cause. Each could make a strong argument for return of the schoolhouses and a portion of the lands. There goes the profit from a potential development. That didn't sit well with Wesley and Neil, who were figuring they could snap those schoolhouses up, especially as the county tax base continues to shrink. Wesley said when we've reached the point where some factions start talk-ing about selling off Yellowstone Park, anything is up for grabs. Neil and Wesley thought they could get the whole package by June of next year. They already had the money, and they removed their two greatest obstacles."

"What matters to humans? Is it always money?" Mrs. Murphy won-dered.

"Money certainly drove Wesley and Neil," Tucker answered.

Cooper continued, "Wesley is already turning against Neil, ob-viously. He says Buddy was out there in the field because he was going to walk to Mount Carmel in costume to scare more people after the last wagon took off. I don't believe it for a minute. Buddy says Wesley offered him another big sum for his land, Buddy refused, and Wesley threatened him. Wesley pulled a gun, Buddy deflected it, then ran out of the schoolhouse. Wesley, shrewdly, called Neil to intercept Buddy. At least that's what I believe. If they killed him, the men figured they could break down Buddy's wife by throwing money at her. After all, being a widow would probably have reduced her income. Wesley swears that when he heard the shots, he fled. He knew Neil had lost it. Once Neil can talk, we'll have his side of the story."

"Idolatrous capital," Harry said, then noticed their blank stares. "Mother used to say that. People worship capital, money. Things are more important than people."

"That's nothing new," Fair quietly said.

"Tazio and Harry really were the last impediments. Tazio might not have been, except they killed Hester. Tazio picked up the torch," Cooper said. "As for Harry, Wesley knew she was on the trail and getting way too close."

Harry said, "Taz's okay, by the way. A knot on the head and the doctors think she might have had a slight concussion, so she has to be a little careful."

"Barry will be fine, too," Coop reported. "He said he heard the dirt bike, heard it stop somewhere behind him, but not close to him. He didn't hear the footsteps, no surprise given all the screams. You know what I think about? They might have gotten away with it. They killed and dressed both Josh and Hester. Wesley says they did it to create confusion, make us think the killer was mad, nuts. But you know, I think they both got caught up in it, the theater of it. It became a high for them. Neil, getting arrogant, figured he could pull this off without too much trouble. Wesley says he tried to talk him out of it, but I doubt he tried too hard."

Cooper exhaled. "Anyway, I expect they've brought about what they most feared. Once all this is out in the open, the public will clamor for Random Row to become a museum. The lynchpin will be Buddy. Will he give up the forty acres that used to belong to the Monacans?"

"Buddy usually does the right thing." Harry stroked Mrs. Murphy's soft fur. "I do think the animals should get something."

"I'll work on it." Cooper smiled.

"You know what surprised me the most?" Harry suddenly said. "Neil and Wesley are Lutherans. *Really.*"

Fair burst out laughing. "Honey, I'm certain Lutherans have committed heinous crimes in the past."

The humans laughed, then Pewter piped up, "*Murphy, see if you can get them to understand you don't want a medal. Tuna! We want tuna and catnip.*"

"*Or bones,*" Tucker remarked.

"*Tuna is better. You can eat tuna. Bones you just chew.*"

"*Pewter, who says I'm going to share?*" Mrs. Murphy replied.

"*Of course you will, because I am your very best friend.*" Pewter purred this with uncommon sweetness.

The tiger cat and corgi just looked at each other.

Finally, Mrs. Murphy said, "*If you promise to help Mom and Tazio fulfill Hester's dream, save the schoolhouses and the land, I will share lots.*"

Without hesitation, Pewter passionately agreed. "*Of course I will. You know very well Mom can't do anything without me.*"

Dear Reader,

The Monacan Indian Nation celebrates an annual powwow usually during high spring. Kathleen King, a friend made way-back-when through basset hunting, often attends. The dancing, food, storytelling, paintings, carvings, baskets, and more underscore this old culture that has survived despite all.

Thanks to Kathleen and her research, I became interested. The federal government's refusal to acknowledge the Virginia tribes took me by surprise. Then I got mad. Perhaps you will, too.

Many nations on earth have subjugated others at one time in their history and often with astonishing brutality. Each government, each nation, has to study its errors and learn from it all, and redress the sorrows where possible.

As Americans we are in a better position than most to do this. We live and work in the light of the Declaration of Independence, the Constitution, and the Bill of Rights.

Let's live up to them.

Always and Ever,

Dear Reader,

While it is true that Kathleen King provided much information, I really did all the work.

Yours,

Dear Reader,
Liar!

The true artist,

Pewter

To Whom It May Concern,
Cats are crazy.

Yours,

Tucker

About the Authors

RITA MAE BROWN has written many bestsellers and received two Emmy nominations. In addition to the Mrs. Murphy series, she has authored *A Nose for Justice* and *Murder Unleashed*, the first two mysteries in a new dog series, and the Sister Jane foxhunting series, as well as many other acclaimed books. She and Sneaky Pie live with several other rescued animals.

SNEAKY PIE BROWN, a tiger cat rescue, has written many mysteries—witness the list at the front of this novel. Having to share credit with the above-named human is a small irritant, but she manages it. Anything is better than typing, which is what "Big Brown" does for the series. Sneaky calls her human that name behind her back, after the wonderful Thoroughbred racehorse. As her human is rather small, it brings giggles among the other animals. Sneaky's main character—Mrs. Murphy, a tiger cat—is a bit sweeter than Miss Pie, who can be caustic.

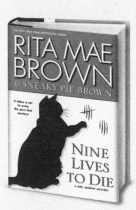